# BLOOD IN THE SNOW

# ALSO BY RYAN PACHECO

Benghazi and Beyond – Isaac Jones #1

Targeted – Isaac Jones #2

(With Dennis Mansfield)

The Heist – Alexander Stone #1

Earth's Dimensions

# BLOOD
## IN THE
## SNOW

*A Novel*

RYAN PACHECO

TEN 41 Publishing

BLOOD IN THE SNOW



Published in the United States of America by Ten-41 Publishing, 10-41 LLC



LIBRARY OF CONGRESS CATALOGING-IN-PUBLICATION DATA
Name: Pacheco, Ryan, author.
Title: Blood in the Snow / Ryan Pacheco
Description: First Edition. – Ten 41 Publishing / Ten 41 LLC [2023]
Subjects: LCGFT: Novels
www.ryanpacheco.us
LCCN: 1-12704816271

Identifiers: ISBN:

Print 979-8-218-14289-6

eBook 979-8-9889869-0-4

9 8 7 6 5 4 3 2 1 0

*For My Sister, Jenny*

# CHAPTER
# ONE

## NORTH IDAHO MOUNTAINS – PRESENT DAY

Kathleen Wood was seated in an oversized wooden chair with fluffy tan and brown oversized cushions in front of the fireplace. Her small log cabin was quietly secluded within a forest on the United States and Canadian border at the tip of Idaho. The heat from the crackling fire warmed her cheeks and hands. Her body was covered with thick outside clothes, warm pants, and a thick snow jacket. She picked up a blue stocking cap and pulled it over her thick brown hair that extended past her shoulders. Her curls bubbled underneath the rim of the cap like a Yo-Yo.

She pulled on her matching blue gloves and stood up, ready to go. It was late, almost midnight, but it was the time of the night she loved the most. She had gotten into the habit of taking a nightly walk in the moonlight to appreciate her surroundings. This was a little piece of heaven on earth.

She lived alone but was rarely lonely. She chose this living situation. The quiet, peaceful oasis she built here was worth the seclusion. In the past, her life had been somewhat chaotic. Well, a lot chaotic. So, the simple life was a blessing, for now. Maybe forever. She hadn't decided yet and was in no hurry to.

The night was overcast with low gray clouds covering the night sky so thick the stars were concealed. Small, light snowflakes had lightly drifted from the sky about a half-hour prior, blanketing the ground like cotton candy.

After a much too short but warm summer, fall had arrived and seemed to be leaving just as quickly. It was only October, but winter showed that it was eager to arrive. There had been a major snowstorm two weeks ago, the first of the season, and it arrived with gusto. Hardly any of the almost two feet of snow that pummeled the area had melted. This wasn't unusual this far north in Idaho, so close to Canada. The locals were used to a short spring, an even shorter summer, a long winter, and an almost nonexistent fall.

Kathleen had cleared her most used walking paths for easier access, but the snowpack around her little cabin remained piled up and was turning into ice bricks. She loved how it resembled a wintry Thomas Kinkade greeting card.

Kathleen walked to the front door and picked up her shotgun from its usual resting place next to the front door. She stepped out into the chilly air, taking in a deep breath through her nose. She savored the sweet smell of the wet, frozen forest, noting that it was uncommonly quiet.

Perhaps the fresh snowfall had sent the wildlife to their homes for the night or caused them to burrow deep to stay warm. She let her breath out through her mouth, watching her breath hover in the air in front of her. It sparkled like a disco ball in the light emitted from the cabin. She listened harder. Completely quiet. *That's quite strange,* she thought.

No owls hooted; there were no distant howls from the coyotes. Nothing. All she detected was the slight sound of dripping water coming off the metal roof as the snow melted from the warmth of the cozy cabin below.

She casually took the two steps off the porch. They loudly creaked with each step, permeating the stillness.

She walked into the front area of the yard, which wasn't really a yard. She had never planted grass or anything else. She let nature choose what would grow and where. She decided the foliage would stay where Mother Nature placed it. She wanted to keep the area's natural feel but also under control, so she spent much of her yard work time trimming, cutting, and pulling out overgrowth.

Over time, she slowly built a walking path made from flat rocks she had picked up on her excursions around her little piece of heaven. The path was mostly finished from the front step, snaking through the yard area to the edge of the woods. There were slight gaps here and there that she still needed to fill with the perfect rocks to match the rest, but she was in no hurry. She enjoyed discovering the right, flat rocks by accident when she wasn't even looking. It made her feel like finding them was meant to be.

She looked toward the moon. The clouds had broken into two pieces and there was a majestic gap between the two largest puffy formations. The nearly full moon lit up the flakes that continued to drift downward like cottonwood seeds that fill the air when the trees shed in the summer. *I love it here.* She smiled to herself as she continued down the walking path.

As Kathleen stepped off the path and entered the woods, she pulled her heavy coat tighter around her body to break the slight chill. It felt ten degrees cooler in the woods. Standing at five-foot-six inches and one hundred thirty pounds, she was in shape, muscular but not ripped like a bodybuilder. Aside from her nightly walks, she liked to jog a mile or so a few times a week. Splitting firewood and keeping up the property kept her strong and healthy, both mentally and physically. She felt good in both areas. It had taken her a while to get there. The hard work and being up in the woods, away from people, had done wonders.

She hadn't seen another person for almost six months. On the rare occasion, she did see someone, it was usually down the mountain in the little store or post office run by her friend, Clint. Surprisingly, she found not being around people very appealing. Many times lately, she would say to herself, "Perhaps I just don't really like people very much."

She was worried when she first got the cabin that she might get too lonely or feel cut off from society. She wondered if she might have to reconsider her choice of living there, but the opposite happened. She loved it. She knew without a doubt it was the right choice.

She left small footprints in the snow behind her as she casually strolled, imprecisely wandering down a slight ravine toward the river. The water was crystal clear like you would see in a spring water commercial. It produced fresh fish for food whenever she was in the mood. The moon was brightly reflected on the river water as if it were a long, squiggly mirror.

Kathleen slowly maneuvered her way and was careful not to slip on the wet ground on her way to the riverbank. She found the large boulder she often sat on as she relaxed watching the water rush by. The three-foot-tall boulder had become one of her best friends. Since she had arrived, she'd spent hours sitting on its smooth surface, warm in the summer and cold in the winter. She and Rocky Balboa, the name she gave her boulder, had had some of the best conversations of her life.

She leaned the shotgun against Rocky and dusted the snow off the top with one hand. She gave herself a boost up and found her normal perch. Looking down at the river she noticed a slight, translucent, thin layer of ice formed around the edge about two or three inches. It looked magical and fragile at the same time. Another wonderful act of nature she never tired of seeing.

She closed her eyes and took a deep breath, concentrating on the smell of the river and the sound of running water. It calmed her as the elements rushed to her senses. She tried to ignore the feeling of unease that tingled her spine.

With her eyes still closed, Kathleen thought about how drastically her life had changed. At times, she felt twice her age with all that she had seen. As a child, she excelled in school. Some of her friends told her that she was obsessed with her studies. Others called her an overachiever. She didn't care. She enjoyed learning. Even at a young age, she never longed for the approval of others. Quite frankly, she couldn't care less about what people thought.

She didn't have many memories before she turned ten years old. That was when her parents died in a car wreck. Kathleen was in the vehicle on the night of the accident but had no memory of it. If she tried hard, she could slightly recall what her parents looked like, but it was foggy. She had no pictures. After the wreck, she went to live with an aunt and uncle for a short time, but before her eleventh birthday, she unexpectedly went into foster care. She was moved from home to home until at age sixteen, she graduated from high school early. She was offered a scholarship to an Ivy League college in another state, and she moved into the dorms without hesitation.

She never saw her aunt and uncle again, and as far as she knew she had no family. She never looked to see if there was family out there. She thought, *I've moved on. You can't miss what you don't know or never had, right?* She wasn't so sure, but that was what she told herself and it made her feel better.

Once she arrived at college, the world was open to her. She could be whatever she wanted: doctor, lawyer, architect, anything. She was very smart, but unlike many young people in ivy league schools, she was indecisive. It was unnerving to commit to a study for the rest of her life. *How could someone be expected to make such a huge decision so early in life?*

Ultimately, she decided to study law, figuring there were many options and directions she could choose from after graduating. Two years into her studies she had a 4.0 GPA, catching the attention of CIA recruiter, John Simon, and her life path was chosen for her. He recruited her, helped her graduate near the top of her class, and signed her up with the agency shortly after her twentieth birthday.

She was sent to Camp Peary in York County, Virginia, also known as, "The Farm." She spent just over six months at the ultra-secret 9,000-acre training base. She became a marksman shooter and learned how to fight, parachute, spy craft, and more. She passed all the mental, physical, and agility tests near the top of her class. Simon was pleased. He frequently boasted, "Can I pick 'em or what?"

When her training was completed, she was assigned to clandestine services in the Middle East, one of the toughest assignments one can get. It's not common for a recruit to get that assignment right out of the gate, but Simon felt she could handle it. He wanted to challenge her and see how she performed.

Toward the end of 1990, Kathleen called it quits. She was assigned to Operation Desert Shield in Iraq, and she'd had enough. She had enough of the stress, death, and destruction that came with a Middle East assignment. She lost many friends and American sentiment was teetering in the area; it was becoming quite unstable.

She was tired of the sand and heat, which might explain why

she chose to live in the American mountains so far north you could almost see Canada from your front porch. She picked a place where the winter occupies more of the year than summer. It was a much-needed change, and she was all in.

Simon told her the CIA did not want to lose her and gave her any choice of assignments. "London? Paris? Russia?" He offered anywhere he could think of that was the opposite of her Middle East assignment. Kathleen declined all of them. She said she needed a break. She needed to recharge her batteries and get her mind straight. She didn't have any family and wasn't in a relationship that would tie her down to any specific place. She just wanted to be free to disappear for a while without anyone or anything tying her down.

She had money. She hadn't spent hardly any of her military earnings, and her 401K and stocks were doing very well. In 1991, the stock market had a huge year-end rally, and the value of her stocks and bonds increased by nearly 20 percent.

She found the cabin with ten acres in northern Idaho for sale at a bargain price. She paid cash and still had money in the bank. Her pension allowed her to live more than comfortably.

The cabin was sparsely used by the previous owners. It was a summer vacation retreat and a winter getaway only a few times a year. It needed many repairs and modifications to make it a full-time residence. She had to replace the old, worn-out wiring and get a more powerful generator, but the septic and water well properly functioned. The bathroom in the cabin was ridiculously small and only held a toilet and linen closet. She pulled the closet down and installed a narrow shower, but she rarely used it since it drained into the septic tank, and she only wanted to empty the tank once or twice a year. In the summer, she bathed in the river.

She found an old-fashioned, deep copper tub with claw feet and put it in the living room to the side of the fireplace, so she could soak in a hot bath next to the fire in cold months. She set the tub up, so the bath water would drain and empty in the woods.

There was no phone or cell service, so she purchased a satellite phone, which she kept activated in case of an emergency.

Kathleen was yanked back to reality by crunching ice and the splash of water. She opened her eyes and scanned both sides of the riverbed. The snow had stopped falling, but she saw nothing. She wondered if she was hearing things, but she instinctively clutched the shotgun.

K athleen stood up with the long-gun in front of her pointing toward the ground. Over the rumbling of the water, she swore she heard a splashing sound, then another.

She looked upstream toward the sound. She almost missed it, but in the moonlight, she saw what she thought looked like a man's head bobbing up and down with the current, coming her way.

She looked harder. *Yes! It is a person in the water. What the hell?*

She knew the river wasn't deep, only about four or five feet this time of year, but it was running swiftly and cold, breathtakingly cold. Questions bombarded her mind in quick succession. *What's he doing in the water? Why is he out this late? What's he doing out here? Who could he be? What should I do?*

The man seemed to be coasting more than floating in her direction. He struggled to keep his head above the furious current. Then his head submerged, and she lost him. After a moment, he reappeared, traveling quickly. He got close enough that she could see the puffs of his breath as they floated in the cold air above him. His eyes were open wide with panic until they rolled back in his head. Kathleen yelled, "Hey! Over here! Swim to me!"

He didn't respond. He didn't even look her way. She set the shotgun down on the ground and looked for something, anything she could find that might help her get him out. She remembered a long tree branch she had used over the summer to dislodge debris and dismantle beaver dams.

She quickly found the stick and raced to the river's edge. She extended it out into the water. It was a struggle to keep the branch out far enough to intercept the man. The strong current wanted to sweep it out of her hands. "Damn it!" she yelled out of frustration.

She held the branch out as far as she possibly could without losing it. She wasn't sure if it would be far enough.

"Grab it!" she yelled.

He seemed to hear her or noticed the limb in front of him. He reached, missing by just inches, and submerged underwater again.

"Damn it!" Kathleen yelled again.

She pulled the limb back out of the water and ran further down the edge. Her footsteps crackled down on the light sheet of ice at the edge of the bank, breaking the picturesque landscape she had been admiring. She slipped on a wet rock and went down hard. Her tailbone screamed with pain and the branch flew from her hands. She saw the man's head come back up. Fighting the pain, she pushed herself up, grabbed the branch, and got as close to the river's edge as she could. She pushed the branch back out, "Swim to it!"

The man managed to paddle his weak arms closer to her. Kathleen struggled to keep the branch in place. He reached and snagged it with one hand.

"Hold on, tight!" she yelled. He seemed to nod as the current crashed into his body. Water covered his face with a swell and then he reappeared. He squeezed his eyes closed.

Kathleen held on to the limb with both hands and walked backward, keeping him visible in case he got washed away again. As she pulled him toward the edge, she noticed he didn't have a shirt on. *Jesus, he's got to be freezing.*

She continued to pull and walk backward until he met the

river's edge. She dropped the branch and sloshed through the water and light ice layers to get closer. Even in the moonlight, she saw his skin was blue. She grabbed his arms and pulled him the rest of the way out of the water. He wasn't just shirtless; he was naked. She was in disbelief. He was in good shape, but if she didn't get him back to the cabin in front of the fire, he would probably die of hypothermia.

She tried lifting him, but his body was too slippery from the river water, and she couldn't get a grip. He was too heavy. There was no way she was going to be able to get him to his feet on her own.

"You must stand up! Help me get you up so I can get you to the fire!"

The man moaned something she couldn't make out.

"Stand up, dammit!"

He lethargically bent his legs and got to his knees. She pulled her coat off and wrapped it around his blue shoulders. She pulled him up by the arm to stand. Their breath clouds filled the cold air in front of them. She finally got him up. He was much taller than her, and the coat barely reached his waist.

"Come on, this way," Kathleen said, guiding him back toward Rocky Balboa. As they passed her rock, she held the man with one arm wrapped around his waist and grabbed the shotgun off the ground with the other. His bare feet slipped numerous times as they climbed the ravine, and she struggled to keep them both from stumbling to the ground.

They quickly cleared the woods and found her rock path, "Just a little further," she said with tired breath. "Slow and steady."

As they reached the cabin and maneuvered up the steps, she kicked the door open. Once inside, she dropped the gun on the floor and led him to the soft rug in front of the fireplace. Unable to hold him up any longer, she let him collapse on the rug. His eyes were closed.

She ran to the hall closet and grabbed some blankets and a dry towel. She pulled her coat off him and used the towel to dry his body and hair. She then covered him with a mound of blankets. She filled a tea kettle with water and placed it on the hook above the fire.

Exhausted, Kathleen collapsed into the wooden chair. She watched the man, wondering who he was and if she did the right thing by bringing him into her home. She picked up the shotgun by the front door and set it down by the chair. She pulled off her outside clothes and threw them into a corner of the room, revealing her jeans and a white T-shirt.

The man was clean-shaven, maybe a few years younger than her, with short, sandy brown hair. He had longer-than-normal sideburns. She watched the color return to his face and his breathing was regulated as he slept. *Attractive?* She wondered. *Perhaps. Relax Kath, a man is the last thing you need around here,* she scolded herself.

She sat in her chair looking at the stranger lying on the floor of her cabin. She detected a slight sense of panic building in the pit of her stomach. She had never had a stranger stumble onto her property before, ever. *What's going on?*

# CHAPTER
# FOUR

## ONE WEEK PRIOR

David Patterson briskly walked down the sidewalk of a comfortable residential area in Berlin, Maryland. He unfoiled a piece of watermelon gum he had purchased at a corner market. The streets were neatly lined with crabapple trees and the songbirds sang happily. As David walked under the tall branches, he noticed that the cool October weather had started changing many of the leaves from greens to beautiful shades of browns, oranges, and reds.

It was cool but not cold, about 50 degrees, and David had his wind-breaker zipped tight around him with his hands in both pockets. He walked past beautiful Victorian-style townhomes and historic houses. Many had been converted into apartments like the building his apartment was in. Up the road and around the corner, David's apartment was in a converted home built in 1910. It had recently been completely remodeled with new paint, new carpet, and new appliances, and had a new_modern feel to it.

He casually hummed Jimmy Hendrix's "All Along the Watch-tower" to himself while he kept a good pace. Not because he was in a hurry but to beat the slight chill coming across him. He took a deep breath, capturing the smell of wet fall leaves.

Traffic was light and moving casually along the street next to him. It was a typical mid-morning day in Maryland, just a stone's throw from the nation's capital.

David's weight and height were so average that if you saw him on the street, you probably wouldn't notice much about him. He looked more like a Californian than a D.C. resident with his bleached blond hair that was slightly longer than most D.C. area political staff would keep. Although it was combed, the cut always had a messy, unkempt look to it. Some might say it was reminiscent of how a 90s grunge band member might keep it but slightly more conservative.

As he rounded the corner toward his apartment, an overwhelming feeling of danger filled his stomach. His unit would say his spidey senses tingled. The short hairs on the back of his neck and the hair on his arms stood at attention like an alarm going off.

He looked toward his building. It looked normal. No one was standing in front or on the red brick steps leading up to the door. There was no doorman. Instead, the door required a swipe card or keypad password to enter.

He quickly scanned the rest of the area, suspiciously eyeing a nondescript white van parked across the street from his apartment building. The van was an older, 1990s Ford Econoline, cargo van. There were no windows on the sides or back other than the driver's and front passenger side doors. He also noted that the van didn't have a back license plate.

David had been around long enough to know this type of van is often used by the CIA for surveillance or when they're on location serving a search or arrest warrant. *Curious*, he thought. He stopped moving forward and stepped back to the corner of a building, providing some concealment and a good vantage point to watch from. He lifted a hand to his chin and nervously rubbed it from side to side.

He pulled his jacket tighter, feeling his shoulder holster snuggle deeper into his side under his right armpit. He wanted confirmation that his 9mm Sig Sauer Pistol was accounted for just in case he needed it. It was not his favorite pistol, but it fit his shoulder holster nicely and he wanted to wear it while he was out.

He was unable to see inside the van due to the blacked-out window tint, but the exhaust plume rising in the cool air from the back of the vehicle clued to him that there was at least one person inside.

He grabbed his phone from his back pocket. He held it in front of his face so the biometrics would unlock it. He tapped the security camera app used for home security located on his home screen. He tapped, "live view" for the camera hidden in the far corner of his living room. It peeked from the top corner of a bookshelf and around a picture frame containing a photo of himself in military greens with his two best pals from the military, Greg Kohl and Kathleen Wood. Greg died in Iraq and Kathleen was living somewhere in the woods in Idaho. He hadn't seen her in a while.

As the camera came online, he nodded to himself, "Yep, there they are." He sighed deeply with concern and worry, but not surprise.

He saw about a half-dozen agents searching through his things. He couldn't tell if they were FBI, Homeland, or CIA, but they were probably CIA since they didn't have the standard FBI look.

They could be Secret Service, but he thought that was doubtful. If this was a response from whom he thought it was, they wouldn't get the Secret Service involved, not yet anyway.

"Shit! I'm burned," he whispered to himself, and he logged out of the app. He put the phone away in his back pocket and turned around slowly, casually, to not to draw any attention. He walked back the way he came, fading into the morning activity. *Time to disappear,* he thought with a look of worry on his face.

David lay on the bed of the cheapest hotel he could find on the outskirts of Arlington, Virginia, near Ronald Reagan International Airport. He wasn't low on money, but he didn't want to use a credit card or give his I.D. to the front desk employee. Credit cards are easy to track, and he didn't want to take any chances.

He knew hotels in this area had no problem accepting cash and required no I.D. You could say people who stayed at places like this valued their privacy, everyone from drug dealers, prostitutes, illegal aliens, and those running from something. This kind of place was a good spot to lie low and be undetected. Watch your back, mind your own business, and you'll be fine.

The decor hadn't been updated since the '70s or early '80s. It had orange and brown checkered curtains, light brown shag carpet, and wood-paneled walls. The desk and TV stand were made of cheap pressed wood and the bed was dressed in a yellow and brown checkered comforter with matching pillowcases. The room was crowned by a large white teardrop lamp hanging from a chain on the ceiling near the bed. The only thing missing was a coin deposit box to make the bed vibrate. David felt as if he had traveled back through time, picturing himself in a DeLorean and turning up the radio to blast Huey Lewis & the News sing, "Back in Time."

After spotting the men searching his apartment, David hired an Uber to take him to Arlington, and he walked to the shoddy hotel, making sure not to do anything that made him stand out or be noticed. He scanned for security and traffic cameras as he walked, shielding his face when necessary either with a fake cough or sneeze or by turning in the other direction away from the cameras.

He needed some time to think and put a plan together. He knew what he had done was risky and extremely dangerous, but he had thought Samuel Harrison would fear his threat, do what he asked, and that would be that. Of course, he was assuming those people in his apartment were working for Harrison, but he needed to confirm it.

Harrison was the sitting president's chief of staff. Harrison was a former CIA boss. His work was mostly classified, and it was the topic of much speculation and rumors in Washington, D.C. Some said he was a deputy director operating under the director of the CIA, but no one could confirm that. Nor did they know which director he worked under. Others said he was a highly sought-after private security contractor and adviser to the American Government during the Gulf War. One thing was certain; he made a lot of money and gained influence and power over the years.

Everyone agreed when discussing Harrison, he must know where the bodies are buried. It's the only way to explain his swift rise in politics over the last few years.

Harrison came across as confident and fearless in a town that rewards falling into step with the establishment and not shaking things up. Keep the status quo; keep the establishment happy. This fearless attitude projected Harrison was the guy who had the dirt and wasn't afraid to use it if it worked to his advantage. Status quo or not, a simple leak of the right information to the right journalist could kill a career. This worried a lot of people, but no one was willing to challenge the man. So his power continued to grow.

When the president appointed Harrison as chief of staff, it sent shockwaves through D.C. It was an appointment that no one saw coming. The town went crazy with rumors about why this man, who wasn't trusted on a bipartisan basis, would get a position with such proximity to the most powerful man in the world. Many wondered what Harrison might have on the president. No one knew.

David knew Harrison from when he was deployed to Iraq. Harrison was known as a CIA liaison at the time, which most took to mean that he was sent there by someone in the CIA but not an employee. If he was CIA, he was a special, special agent. Most likely, he was a civilian contractor. There was more money to be made as a civilian off the war effort than from a government salary. Harrison never hid his affection for the finer things in life.

It was in Iraq that David met Kathleen Wood and Greg Kohl. They became his best friends. They were almost inseparable. After Greg died, he and Kathleen stopped hanging out. It was a tough time for them both. Gregg seemed to be the glue that held the three friends together. Once he was gone, the friendship evaporated without any conversation or talk at all. It just ended.

After their deployments were over, David and Kathleen each went their separate ways. David went to the D.C. area and worked as an adviser to various politicians or special interest groups. He heard Kathleen was living off-grid in a cabin in the high mountains of Idaho, with no cell phone, internet, cable TV, nothing. She was living a simple life. *Good for her*, he thought.

"What was I thinking?" he scolded himself. He didn't ask Harrison for money. David didn't look at it as blackmail. He just wanted some kind of acknowledgment about what they did to Greg in Iraq.

Deep down he knew Harrison was involved, and he probably gave the order. *Why?* He wanted closure so he could finally move on. He would like to say his reasons for taking such a risk were loftier than that. Maybe it would be better to say it was a favor to the American people or Greg's family. It would be noble if David exposed Harrison to the American people, so they would know what kind of people ran the country. Washington, D.C. was full of corrupt politicians and their minions.

He assumed that most people probably wouldn't even be surprised or shocked. He doubted it would even make the nightly news if it were revealed. The rules were different for politicians than for the average American. As wrong as that sounded, society had come to accept it.

Then a new worry came over him. If Harrison figured out who he was, might he think Kathleen was involved too? "Shit!" He had no way to give her a heads-up or warn her. Last he knew she was in Idaho, but was she still? He didn't have any idea how to reach her.

As he thought about what his next step should be, he closed his eyes. *I'm exhausted.* He let out a deep sigh, and before he knew it, he drifted to sleep.

# CHAPTER
# SIX

## LANGLEY, VIRGINIA – CIA HEADQUARTERS

John Simon was one of the many deputy directors at the Central Intelligence Agency. His office was only three doors down from the director. The closer your office is to the director, the more influence you have inside the agency. Being just a few doors down, Simon yielded a lot of power and was not unnoticed by others.

He spent more than thirty years in the United States military; much of that time he supervised clandestine operations around the world. He also oversaw many operations in Iraq during Desert Storm/Desert Shield as well as numerous efforts in multiple African countries. His specialty was identifying and targeting terrorist threats to the homeland.

A few years ago, the director of the CIA personally recruited Simon for the position he held. He had a reputation for being fair but a hard-ass. He was approachable if all your ducks were in a row, but if he sensed someone was unprepared, watch out. His attitude made him a great and worthy adversary. He was not afraid to dress down even the most senior or highest-ranking members of the agency. If someone dared challenge him, they had better not miss their target or there will be consequences. He was rarely challenged, but when it occurred, challengers were often reassigned.

Simon feared no one and couldn't care less about inter-agency politics. He knew all too well that Washington, D.C. was all about power, money, and status. Sometimes those traits conflicted with truth and equal justice.

Many times, people who were supposed to be representing their constituents were old-fashioned, snake-oil salesmen, clinging to power and enriching themselves along the way. Some came with good intentions but didn't realize they had fallen deep into a rabbit hole until it was too late to go back. They were stuck, stuck in the swamp, and once you're in that deep, the swamp doesn't let you go, ever. It was no wonder that Washington D.C. had one of the highest murder rates and missing person rates in the country.

At 9:00 a.m., Simon had already sat in on three security briefings and two asset reviews and was on his fifth cup of coffee.

## WHITE HOUSE – CHIEF OF STAFF'S OFFICE LATER THAT EVENING

Samuel Harrison was standing behind his oversized desk when his cell phone rang. He reluctantly answered knowing he shouldn't have this conversation so close to the oval office. "We lost him, sir," said the voice on the other end.

Harrison slammed the phone down with such force the screen cracked from the top right corner and quickly webbed its way across the screen to the left bottom corner.

"Damn it!" he said out loud. Not because of the damage he had just done to his fairly new iPhone but because of the information he just received.

He collapsed down into the large leather chair just behind him. He smoothed out his khaki pants and straightened the collar on his golf shirt. He rarely wore a suit and tie like many of his predecessors.

Putting his right arm on the armrest, he nervously scratched his chin while deep in thought. He then moved his index and middle fingers to the side of his right cheek and tapped. He learned the technique from a therapy session. It was supposed to be an alternative to treatments like acupressure. He moved his fingers to the side of his forehead and continued to tap whispering out loud, "I am cool and calm. I am cool and calm. I am cool and calm."

He took a deep breath through his nose. He held it and let it out through his mouth.

He leaned forward and picked up his desk phone. His personal assistant picked up, "Yes, sir?"

"Jessica, would you please have a pot of coffee brought in for me, my dear?"

After a slight pause, she asked, "Working late, are we? Did I forget something on the calendar, sir?"

"I have some research to go over before I leave for the night. Nothing to worry about."

Harrison had already let Jessica know about his intention to run for the presidency. He told her so she could make sure he wasn't mixing his current position with campaign work. There had to be a separation, and he needed her help to keep it that way.

"Okay, it's on the way," she told him.

He placed the phone in its carriage and sat back, closed his eyes, and rubbed them with his fingers, trying to stave off a headache.

Many considered Harrison to be a big man, although he was slight in stature at only five-foot-five and one-hundred-and-sixty pounds, it was more regarding his power than his physical presence. Like a young Dustin Hoffman, he had dark hair and well-defined facial features.

This news meant he would have to raise the stakes. That would be tricky and risky. *Story of my life*, he smiled to himself with confidence.

# CHAPTER
# SEVEN

David woke up in the same position he had fallen asleep. His mind was clearer now. *I screwed up. How am I going to fix this?*

He rubbed the sleep out of his eyes and grabbed his phone. He opened an app. Not an everyday app available to the general public. This app was developed by a friend who was *affiliated* with the State Department. Meaning, the friend wasn't officially employed by the United States Government but was an independent sub-contractor.

The app was designed to encrypt text messages; the receiver could only read the message if they had the encryption key. The key must be entered each time a new text was delivered. David composed a text.

He hit send and waited.

About five minutes passed. While lying on the bed, he wondered if he would get a response. David hadn't talked to the man in many years. He then wondered if the app was still updated and functioning. Maybe the person forgot the encryption code.

As David attempted to control the bombardment of worries his mind sent, a ding on his phone let him know he received a response. He let out a sigh and read the short answer.

Marcel's on Pennsylvania Ave. @ 1800 hours.

The suggested meeting place concerned David. Marcel's was a well-known five-star restaurant in D.C. The who's who of success, or those wanting to be seen as a who's who in the power-hungry vortex of American politics, dined and socialized there. Marcel's is a status-symbol restaurant. If you can get a table, and that's a big if, you're in. It's that simple.

The night manager, Jean-Pierre, decided who got tables each night. He scrutinized the reservation list, carefully deciding who gets what table, and choosing who sat next to whom. It was a popularity contest, and he decided who the *cool kids* were and who got to be seen with the cool kids.

For decades, Jean-Pierre has been locked into the political land-scape, and his sources were impeccable. He was connected to everyone from politicians to reporters, gossip columnists to personal assistants, and podcasters to bloggers. Most of the time, Jean-Pierre knew someone's career was over before they did.

He could be considered one of the most powerful people in D.C. politics. Some say he can make or break a political career just by the table he seats you at. If he gives you a table early in your career, you become well-known overnight. On the other hand, if you can't get a table late in your career, you're done, washed up and everyone knows it. In D.C., perception is reality, and it trickles down to everything from committee assignments to cabinet positions.

Knowing not to argue about the suggested location without risking losing the meeting altogether, David simply texted back.

Copy that.

He got ready.

At six, David exited his Uber and slowly crossed the street toward Marcel's. He was met with a warm smile from a blonde hostess named Tina. He was glad it was an early meeting. He scanned the not-yet-full room quickly and told Tina, "I am meeting—"

"Mr. Simon is already here and expecting you, Mr. Patterson. Please follow me," she interrupted.

A curious look stretched across his face as Tina led the way. He'd only been to Marcel's once previously, and that was a few years ago when he was invited by a friend who worked for a political PR firm, so he was a little surprised Tina knew who he was.

They walked past the bar and through the far side of the dining area. The house lights were dim, and smooth piano bar music comfortably filled the room. David recognized a few faces but didn't know anyone personally. He felt a bit like a fish out of water.

He spotted two well-known senators seated at the bar talking with each other. *Interesting,* he thought since one is a Democrat and the other a Republican, and he had seen both spend much of their cable-news appearance time attacking each other.

Seemingly out of nowhere, Jean-Pierre appeared, "That's fine, Tina. Thank you. I'll escort Mr. Patterson from here."

She nodded and excused herself. "This way please, Mr. Patterson," Jean-Pierre said to David. "Mr. Simon is ready for you."

David and Jean-Pierre walked to a private table toward the back of the room which was one of the most secluded in the restaurant. As they approached, David saw that Simon was already seated at the four-person table. He was sipping what appeared to be a Martini with one green olive. "Your table, Mr. Patterson. Your guest, Mr. Simon."

Simon didn't look up as Jean-Pierre pulled a chair out from the table across from Simon for David.

"What can I get you to drink, my friend?" Jean-Pierre asked David.

"I'll have what he's having."

"Very good," Jean-Pierre said, walking away quickly.

"Have to say, I was surprised to get your message today,

David." Simon looked up, from using a table napkin to clean his reading glasses.

"I know. Sorry. But I need your help. I screwed up big time, and I'm not sure I can get myself out. On top of that, I might've put Kathleen in danger, too?"

Simon's eyes clinched as if he had been stung. While he carefully considered his response, he took a generous sip from his drink. He stealthily looked around the room to see if anyone paid attention to their conversation. Not seeing anything concerning, he contemplated his options carefully.

He could simply get up and walk away, not look back and let the chips David had played fall where they will—none the wiser. Or he could listen because deep down he knew that if Kathleen was in trouble, he would need to do whatever it took to keep her safe. In fact, Kathleen's name being brought up was the only thing that kept him from choosing the first option. He didn't owe David a thing. Kathleen was another story.

## THE WHITE HOUSE – CHIEF OF STAFF'S OFFICE

Samuel Harrison picked up his cell phone. As he tapped the "contacts" tab, he slid his finger over the crack snaking down the screen. "Shit!" he hissed to himself. He found the contact he was looking for and tapped on the number.

A male voice answered, "Yes, sir?"

"How are we doing over there? I just got off the line with the other half of your party, and they lost Patterson. I would prefer not to have any more bad news."

"We just landed. It's frickin' cold! Why would anyone want to live out here? The mountains are pretty but Jeeee-zus, it's cold."

Harrison's assistant, Jessica, tapped lightly on the door and came in. She was accompanied by a young lady from the White House kitchen who was holding a silver tray, featuring a tall silver coffee pot with two silver coffee cups. Before he hung up, he said, "Keep me updated."

He looked up at the ladies, "Thank you. Just over there will be fine."

He pointed to the small coffee table next to a short love seat at the far end of the office. The porter placed the tray down on the table without acknowledging the chief of staff and nervously made her way back out the door.

"Thank you, Abby," Jessica said as the young lady passed on her way out. She smiled with a quick nod and left quickly. Jessica began to pull the door shut and paused halfway. She said, "I hope this *research* you're working on has something to do with your nine-to-five job, otherwise, might I suggest you sit down over there, sip on some coffee and wait another half-hour before you begin doing whatever it is you're planning on doing. I don't have anything on your calendar this evening."

Harrison eyed his faithful assistant, knowing she was right to caution him. "I hear ya. Oh, by the way, I'm going to need a new cell phone please."

"What's wrong with the one you've got?" she inquired.

"Screen cracked," he said holding it up for her to observe.

"Mmm hmm. That's the third one in about as many months." Jessica smiled and winked at her boss. She closed the door.

# CHAPTER
# EIGHT

## MARCEL'S RESTAURANT, WASHINGTON, D.C.

Restaurant manager, Jean-Pierre returned to the table, interrupting David and Simon, who were speaking in hushed tones. He had a waitress in tow. "Excuse us, gentlemen."

The waitress set the Martini down in front of David. "Thank you, Penny, and let's get another for Mr. Simon," Jean-Pierre ordered.

"Right away," she said with a smile.

"Are we going to be having dinner tonight, gentlemen?" he asked, holding up two menus.

Simon jumped in to reply first, "You know your prime rib is my favorite, but I told you that I wouldn't keep the table too long since I didn't have a reservation. So, drinks will be just fine. We shouldn't be too much longer, and thank you for accommodating us."

"Ah, Mr. Simon, you know I will always find a table for you. If you would like dinner, we can certainly accommodate you," Jean-Pierre volleyed.

"You're too kind, but no."

"Very good." Jean-Pierre slightly bowed his head and excused himself.

The two men sat in silence for a beat. Simon finished his drink just as Penny returned with a fresh one. She sat it in front of him, collected the empty glass, and quickly left the men in private.

"So, David? Tell me what's going on."

David let a deep sigh escape his lips. "You remember when me, Kath, and Greg were all stationed together at the Hamptons in Iraq?"

The Hamptons in Iraq was one of Saddam Hussein's palaces the military took over. The military used many of Saddam's palaces for command staff residences, top adviser meetings, supply chain inventories, deliveries, and other logistical activities.

Simon knew exactly what David was talking about since he was in and out of Iraq during the Gulf War. "Yes, David. I remember. That's where I met you and Greg. I already knew Kathleen."

David opened his mouth to continue, but Simon interrupted his thought, "David, please tell me this doesn't have anything to do with Greg's death."

A worried look crossed David's face. Simon continued, "David, I told you back then to let it go. It was an unfortunate circumstance."

"Greg did not commit suicide, John!"

Simon looked around to make sure the conversation wasn't creating unwanted attention. The bar area was full but most of the dining room tables were still empty since the dinner rush hadn't started yet. No one was paying attention to the men. Simon scolded David. "Keep it down. Tell me what you did."

"You know all the cash that was funneling through that building and all the skimming that was going on."

Simon nodded.

David continued, "It was supposed to be used to pay off tribal elders and local leaders to buy cooperation. This isn't anything new. We do it all the time. The difference was that there was never any accounting, John. Millions and millions of cash, wrapped up in plastic sitting on countless numbers of wooden pallets, stacked in a corner at the Hampton's in Iraq. I've never seen anything like it. To this day, no one can tell you where all that money went."

"David, this happens all the time. It still happens today, all over the world. It's nothing new. We send cash everywhere. What did you do?"

"You know we saw everyone, including Americans skimming the money. High-ranking military brass and politicians lined their pockets. They used it like their own bottomless ATM. They took millions of that cash."

"I know that. Everyone knows that happened. We talked about it at the time. Do you remember what I told you then?"

David said, "You told me to stay in my lane and not to worry about things I have no control over. The battle was not worth the fight. That it was a career ender because too many people, powerful people, were dipping into that pot."

"That's right. Pick your battles wisely and don't try to control the uncontrollable."

"Well, I'm not in the military anymore."

"Okay?"

"Samuel Harrison," David finally said.

"The president's chief of staff?"

"Yes."

"And? David?"

"I sent him the video Kath, Greg, and I took of him and others in Iraq skimming the cash."

"You sent him a video? Why the hell would you do that?" Simon asked.

"The man doesn't deserve to be President of the United States. I heard he was about to announce his intention to run, and I wanted to stop his campaign before it got started."

Simon put one hand to his forehead, closed his eyes, and let out an exhausted-sounding sigh. "David." He paused in thought, then he said, "Harrison is a dangerous man. His hunger for power is well known. He will do whatever it takes to make a run at the

White House. Did you really think he would back down? No way in hell. It would never happen. How does Kathleen play into this?"

"Well, I'm not positive, but I implied it when I sent Harrison the video. I told him *we* have multiple copies of the video."

"Why would you say that?" Simon demanded.

"So he'd think that getting to *me* wouldn't eliminate the problem."

Simon said, "So all he had to do was check your service records and see who you were stationed with—who your friends were and who was also at the Hamptons. It wouldn't be difficult to come up with Kathleen."

David sipped his drink and looked down at the table, avoiding Simon's eyes, knowing he was right.

"You not only put a huge target on your back, but you probably put a target on hers as well. Does she know?"

"I don't know how to get in contact with her. That's why I'm talking to you. We need to warn her. Just in case."

"Just in case? It's a guarantee. If they know who you are, they know who Kath is."

David asked, "Do you know how to get in contact with her?"

"Yes. I wish you had asked me before making this monumentally stupid decision. I wish you would have more carefully considered the high stakes and ramifications. Blackmailing Samuel Harrison? Good Lord! I would have told you, do not do it!"

David didn't respond; he knew Simon was right.

# CHAPTER
# NINE



## LANGLEY, VIRGINIA – THREE DAYS AGO

Simon put David up in a secure, off-the-grid location and told him to stay put and keep quiet. Total blackout. Unplugged. No calls, no social media, no nothing. "And damn it, David, you better listen to me this time," he ordered.

It was late and everyone was gone for the day at CIA headquarters. Using his personal satellite phone, Simon attempted to contact Kathleen on her sat-phone number to no avail. He decided that time was not on their side. He was going to have to send someone directly to her. He considered his options. None were ideal. *It has to be off-the-books.* He changed phones and sent a cryptic text from his personal cell to an anonymous number that simply read:

> New orders. Same place as last time. 2200 hours.

No sooner had he pressed send, than he got a thumbs-up emoji reply.

Two hours later, he was parked on the side of the road in the warehouse district, an area most would not feel safe passing through, let alone parking in. Simon wasn't concerned. He was armed with his agency-issued handgun. The dark-tinted windows on the company sedan had a reinforced body, and the windows were bulletproof.

Just as he checked his watch, he heard a tap on the passenger side window. He flinched slightly. Through the window, he could see his contact lean over, looking back at him. Simon clicked the unlock button, and the man opened the door and sat down.

The contact was above average in height, and his clothes clung to his physique, indicating that he was in good shape. He had sand-colored hair, blue eyes, and neatly groomed sideburns that extended past his ear lobes, a look not often seen these days.

Simon said, "Hello, Elvis."

"Very funny. I told you. I like them, and I'm not shaving them off."

"And I told you that the first rule of clandestine work is to blend in. Those hardly blend in."

Despite his position in the CIA, this man was not intimidated by Simon in the slightest. "You're welcome to take your business elsewhere, but I assume if you're calling me, your choices are limited. So, you need me. Right?" He grinned wide. "Lay it on me, old man."

"I need your help," Simon acknowledged. "And I don't have time to shop around, so you'll have to do, Chase."

Chase faked a hurt feelings face and said, "Wow! Warm and fuzzy as usual. So, what's on your mind, pops?"

"Pops? You're lucky I like you. Why I like you, I can't figure it out. "

Chase Osborn wore a big grin of satisfaction. About ten years ago, he was a former recruit of Simon's. Chase worked in clandestine services for Simon before quitting and going out on his own. He was now a private contractor. Someone they call when a mess needs to be cleaned up off-the-books unofficially.

Simon had used Chase for different operations a dozen or so

times over the last few years, and he always delivered good results.

Simon filled Chase in on everything David told him and the worry about Kathleen. He also told Chase that Kathleen was currently living off-the-grid in the mountains of Northern Idaho in a cabin near the Canadian border.

"So, what exactly are you asking me to do?" Chase asked.

"I want you to get to her before they do and warn her."

"You want me to deliver a message in the mountains of Idaho with winter approaching? There's probably already snow on the ground."

"She's a former CIA operative; she can take care of herself, but she needs to know to expect it, so she's not caught off guard. And if she needs to be moved to a secure location, I need you to take care of that, too."

"What if she is unreceptive? I mean, you don't live out in the middle of nowhere on some of the snowiest mountains in the country if you want to be told what to do or where to go. Besides, I hate cold weather."

"Just tell her that I sent you and it's about The Hamptons in Iraq. She'll understand."

"I don't know, Simon. Mountains, cold. The president's chief of staff? And now you drop Iraq into the scenario. I'm not thinking this is going to be as easy as just delivering a message. Man, I'm not sure I'm the guy for this assignment."

"I'll double your normal rate."

Surprise covered Chase's face. Simon had never paid a dime more than the standard rate for a job. He always tried to lowball him on price. Chase must have understood this was important because he relented. "Okay, it's your dime and you don't have to pay double. Standard rate is fine; just throw me some extra business now and again."

Chase opened the door and began to step out just as Simon grabbed his arm. "Chase, this might be nothing, but if it turns into what I think it is, this could be extremely dangerous. Harrison is a powerful man with a lot of resources. Be careful."

Chase said, "I'll take care of her. Text me the coordinates of her cabin. I'll head that way right away. Don't worry. I'll get her."

"Thank you. Text me every twenty-four hours, so I know you're still operating. If you miss a check-in, I'll assume something went wrong."

"Copy that."

Chase quickly disappeared down the road.

# CHAPTER
# TEN



Kathleen slowly opened her eyes. After a short catnap, she shivered and looked toward the fireplace. The fire had died down to a few red coals, and she shivered from the crisp temperature in the cabin. *I must have dozed off,* she thought.

She noticed her visitor had not moved. He was still under the pile of blankets and his head rested on the soft pillow she had given him from her bed. She grabbed a few pieces of split wood from the pile on the side of the fireplace and quietly placed them on top of the coals. The wood sparked and quickly caught fire. Kathleen instantly felt the warmth on her face from the fresh flames. She hadn't shaken the worry away about having a stranger in her home.

She scrutinized the man sleeping under the blankets, noticing beads of sweat pocking his forehead and cheeks. She felt his face. *He's burning up!* The sweat from his face and hair had dampened the pillow. He slightly shivered but remained asleep.

Kathleen dashed to the kitchen and grabbed a white rag off the linen shelf. She poured cold water on the rag and returned to the man, wiping his face, then placing the washcloth on his forehead.

The man opened his eyes slightly, seemingly trying to focus. He gazed at Kathleen, turning his head slightly to one side as if determining whether he recognized her. He shook his head.

"Are you cold?" Kathleen asked, pulling the top of the covers up tight toward his chin.

The man shook his head, lifting an arm and pushing the covers down revealing his chest. Kathleen touched his chest with her hand. It was damp, too, "You're burning up," she told him.

He nodded and through a whispery breath said, "Too hot."

Kathleen ran to the kitchen and retrieved a glass of water. "You should drink some water."

She helped him sit up and lean forward. She set the damp rag on the floor and placed the glass to his lips. He took two small sips and collapsed.

Kathleen placed the glass on the floor next to the rag and reached for the teakettle from the hook above the fire. She went to the copper tub, pushed the plug, and poured the steamy water. She then went to the kitchen and filled a white five-gallon bucket with water and poured it into the bath. She continued this process of one hot kettle with one bucket of cool water until the tub was mostly full. She checked the temperature. It was cool but not frigid.

She knelt beside the man.

Feeling her presence, he opened his eyes.

She told him, "I've drawn a cool bath for you. We need to get your temperature down. Can you get up?"

The man attempted to sit back up. Kathleen caught him with both hands by the shoulders before he fell. She pulled him back up into a seated position.

He shook his head.

"You must get up, and I'm not strong enough to lift you. Try harder. We have to try to break the fever," she ordered.

He nodded.

She let go of his shoulders, "Don't fall back." She pushed the pile of blankets off him.

He swayed back and forth slightly as if only partially awake. His eyes were half shut. Beads of sweat had returned to his forehead and his chest. The man's chin slumped downward.

Kathleen said, "C'mon, get up. It's not far. The tub is right there by the fire. She stood, got behind him, and put both arms under his armpits, attempting to pull him to his feet.

The man leaned forward, and Kathleen used his momentum to push him to his hands and knees. He swayed from side to side but balanced enough not to fall over.

Kathleen did all she could to keep him stable. "Come on. Stand up. I won't let you fall."

Slowly, from his hands and knees, he lifted one foot at a time and unsteadily stood. Kathleen wrapped her right arm around his waist and balanced them both by holding her left arm out to her side.

"Three or four steps and we'll be there. Come on, easy does it. Just one step at a time."

Stumbling, they made it to the side of the tub. The naked man put one hand on the high side of the copper tub to steady himself.

"It's ok, I've got you," Kathleen said, keeping her arm around his waist. "Can you lift your left leg over?"

The man attempted to lift his leg. He lost his balance and started to fall back. Kathleen reacted automatically, releasing his waist. She steadied him with one hand on his shoulder, and with the other, guided him by his glutes. She quickly moved her hand to his thigh to avoid the awkwardness of holding the stranger's butt.

The man was able to steady himself. With both feet on the ground and both hands on the side of the tub, he remained balanced.

He swallowed hard, and his face flushed a bit deeper red than what the fever caused.

She placed one hand on the small of his back and the other on the back of his thigh and pulled the left leg up and over the side of the tub.

He didn't resist.

If the situation was not so serious, Kathleen would have chuckled at the comedic clumsiness. She quickly switched sides and helped maneuver the other leg into the tub.

With both legs in the water, he sat on the side of the tub, and she was able to slowly lower him into the water. The walls of the tub were high, and the back had a good slant allowing for a comfortable recline. He relaxed and closed his eyes for a quick second. A slight smile graced his lips.

Kathleen smiled back, then let out a winded, uncontrolled giggle, "How about another drink of water?"

He nodded and said, "Yes, please."

She pressed the glass to his lips.

He lifted his hand and took the glass, "I can do it." He finished off the rest of the water and gave it back to her.

"Want more?"

"No, I'm good," he said weakly.

Kathleen set the glass down and then scooted her big wooden chair closer to the tub. She sat on the arm trying to not gawk at his muscular body through the water, "Are you feeling better?"

"Yes, the cool water feels good."

"Well, you look better, and you're finally talking."

"I almost fell. Thank you."

She blushed. "It's okay. I caught you by the butt," she said through a laugh.

"Yeah, not my proudest moment." He chuckled, restraining a cough.

She looked away as if trying to find somewhere else to look and didn't reply.

He said, "I think you saved my life tonight. There's no way I would have made it out of the river without your help. Are you all right?"

She allowed her eyes to meet his. Everything had happened so fast that she hadn't had a chance to even think about it. She finally said, "I'm not sure. What's going on? What are you doing out here? How did you get into the water?"

"I'm hungry," he said, avoiding the barrage of questions.

"I have some left-over soup from dinner. I'll start warming it for when you get out."

She got up and went to the kitchen. She hung the soup-filled Dutch oven on the tea kettle hook over the fire. She glanced back at the man.

*Was this a mistake?* she wondered.

# CHAPTER
# ELEVEN

Kathleen took the heated Dutch oven of soup from the fire to the kitchen. The room was filled with the smell of homemade cooking. She loaded a bowl and set it on the counter to cool. She walked back to the tub where the man was shivering again. "Are you cold?"

He nodded.

She felt his forehead, "You still have a temperature."

He grabbed one side of the tub as if to lift himself out, and he slipped back down. "I'm freezing now."

She went to the bathroom and retrieved a fresh bath towel. Standing in front of the tub, she ordered, "Give me your arm. I'll help lift you. Sit on the side, and I'll help you swing around and out."

He nodded.

She grasped his wrists and pulled.

Slowly, he was able to rise. He sat on the side of the tub with his back facing out and his legs in the water.

She moved behind him just before he began to fall back. She caught him under the arms, and he tumbled back into her chest, soaking her t-shirt with water from his skin. "I've got you," she said.

She steadied him and moved to his side, holding onto one shoulder. She lifted one of his legs out of the water, maneuvering him into a turn. As the other leg came around, she lifted it out. Facing her, he was seated on the tub with his feet on the ground. She held on to one leg and retrieved the towel. She dried his legs and feet and wrapped the towel around his shoulders pulling it snugly.

"Can you stand?"

He nodded through a shiver.

She put an arm around his waist and lifted him off the tub. They slowly made their way back to the rug, and she helped him down. Once he was seated, she pulled the towel off his shoulders and dried his back, chest, and hair. She helped him lay back and rest his head on the pillow. She pulled the blankets back over him up to his chin.

He closed his eyes.

"Are you still hungry?" she asked.

He didn't answer.

She felt his forehead again. He was warm, but not as warm as before.

"Are you sleeping?" she whispered.

He didn't answer.

She sighed and went to the kitchen. She dumped the contents of the bowl back into the Dutch oven. When she placed the bowl in the sink, she caught her reflection in the window and gasped. Her t-shirt was soaked to her braless chest. She ran to the bedroom and pulled the wet shirt off and pulled on an oversized sweatshirt that was lying on her bed.

As Kathleen walked toward the doorway into the living room, she thought she saw something moving outside the bedroom window.

She instinctively ran to the living room, picked up her shotgun, and stood by the door, listening. She heard nothing. She looked back toward the fireplace. The man hadn't moved. He appeared to be asleep. She glanced out the window and didn't see anything. She went to the kitchen and looked out that window. Nothing.

She grabbed a flashlight off the shelf and put it in her back pocket. She racked a round in the shotgun and went to the front door. She slowly opened it, searching for threats. She didn't see anything. She wondered if her mind was playing tricks on her.

With the barrel leading the way, she crept onto the front steps. She scanned the woods. She still didn't see or hear anything. She closed the door and lightly crept down the steps. She pulled the flashlight out of her back pocket and turned it on, shining the light on the perimeter of the house. Still nothing. The forest was quiet, and the air was crisp. The sky's faint red and purple tone blended with the black darkness. She knew the sun would be coming up soon.

Once she reached the outside of her bedroom window, she stopped, inspecting the ground. There were no footprints and nothing out of the ordinary. "You just spooked yourself, Kath. Calm down," she whispered.

She flashed the light out into the woods, then around the sides of the house once more. All looked clear. Absolutely no sign of anyone being there.

Satisfied, she returned to the cabin, locking the front door behind her. She leaned the shotgun against the wall and went to the kitchen, putting the flashlight back on the shelf.

She looked back at the man. He hadn't moved. She let out a deep sigh of relief, and then she looked down and froze.

Wet footprints led from the front door to the unconscious man. She crept back to the shotgun and picked it up, holding it close to her body. She leaned against the door, feeling with one hand for the lock on the handle, confirming it was locked. *What the hell is going on?*

She hurried to her bedroom and got her Glock 9mm from under a stack of shirts in the closet. She left the shotgun and returned to the living room.

The sun was beginning to rise, and a very faint morning glow pushed through the windows. Nothing was moving outside. *What the hell is going on?* she asked herself again.

She stationed herself in the big chair next to the tub, staring at the man lying on the floor. She set the pistol down on the armrest next to her. "What have you gotten yourself into?" she asked him. "And what have you gotten me into?"

The man rustled and rolled over, facing away from her toward the fire. The covers slid off, exposing most of his body. She got up and pulled the thinnest blanket from the pile and covered him with it.

*I've got to find him some clothes,* she thought. He was much taller than her, and she doubted her shirts would fit over his broad shoulders. He rolled back over. She felt his forehead again. The fever must have broken, his temperature felt normal.

Slowly, his eyes opened, and he smiled up at her. "You're still here."

"I live here, remember?" She smiled back. "Are you feeling better?"

"Yes."

"I think the fever is gone."

"That's good."

"What's your name?" she asked.

"Chase."

"Hi, Chase. I'm Kathleen."

He pulled an arm out from under the blanket, and they shook hands.

"Care to tell me what's going on?" she asked.

"Long story."

"Someone was in here," she whispered.

"In the cabin?" he asked with a concerned tone.

She nodded.

Chase shot up, "When?"

"Just a little while ago. I thought I saw someone outside. I went out to check and when I returned, there were wet footprints from the front door to where you were sleeping."

He spotted the pistol on the armrest. "Do you know how to use that?"

"Yes."

"Where's the shotgun?"

"In my room."

"You might want to bring it in here."

"What's going on? Who's after you? Why were you in the water? Where's your clothes?"

"Slow down. I'll tell you everything, but you need to get that shotgun right now."

# CHAPTER
# TWELVE

Kathleen returned to the living room and placed the shotgun against the chair next to Chase. She added a few pieces of wood to the fire and returned to her chair. "Ok, I'm listening."

"All right. I came here—"

Chase was cut off by the front door crashing open. Wood splintered from the frame and the small colored glass windows that framed the top half shattered, sprinkling little pieces all over the floor. A tall, beefy man with a red beard clothed in camouflage burst into the cabin with an AR-style rifle.

Kathleen reacted, instinctively grabbing the handgun. She faced the threat. The man rushed toward them, pointing his gun at Chase. Kathleen was about to fire when she heard a loud bang from behind her. The man flew backward as a shotgun slug impacted his chest. He slid across the floor toward the door, sweeping wood splinters and glass with him. Kathleen pivoted to see Chase, who was standing with the shotgun in his hand.

He motioned with his head toward the door. "I'll cover him. Secure his gun and see if he's breathing."

Kathleen nodded, moving toward the man.

"Careful. He might not be the only one. Keep your eyes open," Chase cautioned.

Kathleen picked up the man's rifle and slid it toward Chase. As she inched closer to the man lying on the floor, Chase slowly moved forward, covering the doorway with the shotgun at eye level.

"Watch your step. There's glass everywhere," she warned as Chase approached from behind her.

Feeling for a pulse and finding none, she told Chase, "We might have just found you some new clothes."

"I was just thinking the same thing." He continued to cover the doorway, probing for any other threats.

"He's dead. Do you recognize him?" Kathleen asked.

Chase didn't answer.

Kathleen unfastened the dead man's belt, removed his pants, and held them up. "New pants. I'll wash the blood out and they should fit."

Chase nodded.

"Do you want his underwear, too?" she asked without seriousness.

"No, thanks. I'll be fine." He gave a weak smile, not being distracted by the seriousness of the situation.

Kathleen put the pants in the sink. She then went to the fire and took the teapot from the hook and poured hot water into the sink along with some soap. She grabbed a blanket and wrapped it around Chase as he held his position with the shotgun positioned in a low-ready. The cold morning air rushed in from the doorway, and all the warmth from the cabin was escaping.

"I'll check outside," she said moving toward the destroyed entry point.

"You stay, I'll check," he told her.

"You're naked! And your fever just broke. I don't need you to catch pneumonia. Listen, I'm not sure what's going on or what you've dragged me into, but once things settle down, I need to know! Understood?"

Chase nodded.

She told him again in a don't-argue-with-me tone, "I'll check outside."

Chase nodded.

She walked out of the cabin with the handgun gripped in both hands, keeping her eyes open for threats. She slowly descended the steps and circled the cabin. The sunrise was almost complete, and aside from the frigid temperature, it was a beautiful morning. The cloudless sky was a bright blue. The sun felt warm on her rosy cheeks.

She completed the circle around the cabin finding no additional threats. *Could this guy have been alone,* she wondered. Thoughts bombarded her mind. *It doesn't make sense. They're trying to kill Chase. But why?*

As she returned inside with no answers to her questions, she found Chase seated in the chair by the fire. He pulled a boot onto his foot. The other boot was already on. She looked over at the barefoot dead man on the floor.

"They fit perfectly! What are the odds?" Chase wrapped the blanket around his shoulders.

She studied Chase boldly standing in front of her wearing boots and a blanket.

She couldn't hold back a grin and a nervous laugh. "It's a start." She used a hand to unsuccessfully wipe the grin from her face.

Chase turned a complete circle as if he were modeling the outfit. He smiled and did a quick one-foot tap-dance in his new boots.

Moving on, Kathleen told him, "I didn't see anything outside."

"Footprints?"

"Just his and mine."

"Okay."

Kathleen went into the kitchen and put the gun on the counter and started rinsing the blood out of the pants in the sink. She directed Chase, "See what you can do about that door. It's going to freeze again tonight."

"What should we do with him?"

"After I get these pants washed and hung to dry, I'll get the wheelbarrow and dump him in the river."

Chase checked the man's shirt pockets. They were empty. Blood got all over his hands.

"Do you recognize him?" Kathleen asked.

"I've seen him before."

"He was pointing his gun right at you when he came in."

Chase didn't reply.

"Why did he want you dead?"

Chase walked into the kitchen and put his hands in the water to wash off the blood. He stood close to Kathleen. She looked up at his face. He met her eyes, still washing his hands. He gently said, "It's not me. That guy was here for you, Kathleen."

Kathleen dropped the pants into the sink while she digested what he just told her. She had a curious look and asked, "Me? Why? And how would you know that?"

"That's why I'm here. John Simon sent me to warn you. Unfortunately, they got up here first and caught me before I could warn you."

"What are you talking about?"

"It's true, Kathleen."

"John Simon? My old boss? What does he have to do with this?"

"You know where he works?"

She nodded, "CIA? So? I still don't understand."

"I'm just doing what I was sent here to do. I don't have all the information, but Simon wanted to make sure you were safe and sent me up here."

Kathleen nodded but still didn't understand. She asked, "How did you get into the river?"

"I think they caught my trail north of Bonners Ferry. About a mile from the river, four men ambushed me at a convenience store.

When I came out, two of the men stopped me and two guys drove up in a Hummer. The man in the front passenger seat pointed a gun at me and told me to get in. One of the guys behind me stepped around and opened the back door. They had me, so I did what I was told.

"It's like they knew I was coming, or they knew someone would be coming to warn you. Anyway, we drove for a while up the mountain. They took me to some old broken-down barn. They stripped me of my clothes and tied me up. I guess they figured the likelihood of me trying to escape naked was low in these elements. I'd freeze to death quickly.

"Three of them left me alone with the fourth. The fourth man started a fire, but I was freezing. I asked the guy if I could have a blanket. He told me no. I said I was going to freeze to death, and he said he'd move me closer to the fire. He was untying my hands from the plank when I hit him hard in the face with my forehead. I heard his nose break, and blood went everywhere. While he was stunned and couldn't see, I pushed past him and ran.

"It was snowing, and the ground was so cold. I figured the other three must have been after you, so I ran. But when I was almost to the river, I heard them behind me. The guy from the barn must have contacted the others and let them know I was on the run. I assume they didn't shoot because they didn't want you to hear the shots and get spooked.

"When I got to the riverbank, I looked back and could see their flashlights, so I just jumped in. I didn't expect the water to be so cold. I planned to swim across, but I lost my breath and instantly got disorientated. The next thing I remember is you pulling me out and then waking up in here next to the fire."

Kathleen's mouth dropped open. She raised her eyebrows and in a shaky voice said, "Wow! That's a lot."

The wheels in her head turned. She asked, "But why are they after *me*?"

"I'm not sure it's my place..." Chase trailed off.

"Oh, c'mon!" she demanded.

"Kathleen, I have very limited information. I took a job."

Kathleen pointed to the dead man on the floor, "Is this one of the guys from the barn?"

"Yes."

"That means there are three more out there… somewhere."

Chase nodded.

Kathleen wasn't happy with the lack of information. She felt heat rising in her cheeks.

"I was supposed to save you, but you seem to have saved me first," Chase said.

Kathleen wrung the water from the pants and laid them next to the fire to dry.

"So, why are they after me?"

"Simon said you would know."

"I have no idea."

"He said to tell you, 'The Hamptons in Iraq.' He said that you would know what it meant."

She stepped back and stumbled into a chair. She knew exactly what that meant. Her past was catching up to her.

Just then, a glass bottle with a lit rag hanging from the top flew through the open doorframe. The bottle smashed on the ground next to the dead man, engulfing the floor in flames.

Kathleen and Chase exchanged looks. "Shit!" they both said in unison.

# CHAPTER
# THIRTEEN

Kathleen and Chase sprinted through the bedroom to the back of the house. She had just enough time to grab her jacket and the handgun; he had just enough time to grab the still-damp pants, belt, and shotgun. They crashed through the bedroom window as flames engulfed the entire front of the cabin.

Kathleen contemplated grabbing the sat-phone too, but there simply wasn't enough time.

Outside the back of the house, bullets splintered the cabin and splattered the surrounding ground. They dove for cover. During a brief lull of gunfire, Chase and Kathleen were able to spot two subjects crouched behind the wood pile about fifty yards away. The cabin was completely ablaze. The intense heat was becoming unbearable, and smoke was swallowing the once-blue sky.

"We're either going to burn up or the cabin will fall on us!" Chase yelled, cinching the pants around his waist with the belt. He was still bare-chested.

Kathleen looked over her shoulder. Her small tool shed was about forty yards away to the west.

"The shed!" she shouted, motioning with her head.

"I'll cover you. Go!" he told her.

Chase sprang up, firing toward the men at the woodpile. Kathleen leaped to her feet and ran toward the shed. She pulled the door open and dove in. She propped the door open with a bucket and fired more shots toward the woodpile. Under Kathleen's cover, Chase quickly made his way to the shed. Once inside, he slammed the door shut as a volley of bullets splintered the door and side of the shed. The thin wood was no match for the bullets. The door sprung open again as the latch disintegrated from the gunfire. "We're not going to last long in here," Chase told her. "I'm out of shells."

Kathleen motioned with her head as she returned fire from the now open door, "Back wall, in the gun safe, combo is 911. There should be a box of slugs and grab a box of 9mm for me."

Chase opened the safe and got a box of shotgun slugs, shoving them into his pocket. He found a box of 9mm rounds and tossed it to Kathleen. "Heads up!"

She caught the box and Chase maneuvered himself to her position while he loaded shells. There was a pause in firing from both sides. "I guess we're all reloading," he said.

He knelt next to Kathleen as she loaded her magazine. He handed her two empty 9mm mags he found in the safe, "Might as well load these too. I think we're going to need them."

Kathleen nodded and asked, "Recognize those guys?"

Chase nodded. "I think they're my friends from earlier." Chase sprung up. He lifted the shotgun over Kathleen's head and shot two rounds out the doorway.

Kathleen peeked through the door and saw a large man lying on the ground just outside the shed with a gaping hole in his chest.

"One left," Chase said. "Or two but, probably one."

They both crouched, looking out the doorway for any remaining threats. There was no movement at the wood pile or anywhere around the property that they could see. They carefully checked the area. When they thought they were clear, Kathleen looked over at her now-destroyed cabin which had been reduced to a smoldering pile of soot on top of a concrete foundation. The rock chimney was the only structure still standing. She spotted the bathtub by the fireplace and the kitchen sink, which was now resting on the ground covered in soot.

"My cabin," she sighed. Her shoulders slumped in defeat.

"I'm sorry."

Kathleen looked down, pulling back her tears. Then she looked at Chase. "We've got to get out of here. I need to talk to Simon and find out what's going on." She surveyed the area. "I think the last guy bugged out."

"Let's hope so," Chase answered.

Kathleen went back inside the shed. Chase followed. She took out a thick green winter jacket with a fur-lined hood from a cupboard above the safe and threw it to Chase. "It's going to be a little too small, but it's better than nothing. I don't have any shirts out here, so it will have to do for now. If we can make it down to Cliff's supply store, we should be able to find you some warm clothes that actually fit."

Chase pulled on the jacket. "Just when I was getting used to running around naked. It's so liberating."

"You don't want to get used to it out here this time of year. Frostbite can be painful."

Chase shivered at the statement. "That's a scary thought."

"Simon told me to check in with him every twenty-four hours, and I'm late. He's probably assuming we ran into some trouble and he's sending help." Chase told her as he pulled on the much too-small jacket. He struggled with the tight fit. He could only get the coat to zip a quarter of the way due to his broad shoulders.

Kathleen smiled, watching him fight the zipper.

Making no further progress, he gave up. "Maybe I'll be a trend-setter. Make it cool for guys to wear baggy pants with ladies' jackets two sizes too small."

"I highly doubt that new trend will take off." Kathleen snickered and then felt her face fall. "Simon won't send anyone up here. It's gotten too messy for him to be officially involved. That's why he sent you in the first place. Isn't it? You were the only shot. He'll probably contact local authorities and have them watch for us or possibly come up to the cabin and check on us, but officially, don't count on it."

"Or, he may cut his losses and forget everything. Me, you, forget knowing any of this happened." Chase suggested.

She didn't respond. She collected the rest of the extra ammo, stuffing the boxes in her pockets. She peered out the door. "Let's go, trendsetter."

As they walked out of the shed, Chase asked, "How far to the supply store?"

"About ten miles."

"That's a long walk."

"I prefer driving," she said rounding the shed.

Just then, Chase spotted an older model Jeep Cherokee with side panels parked behind the shed. Chase smiled and got into the front passenger seat, resting the shotgun next to him. Kathleen sat in the driver's seat. She turned the key, and the engine roared to life.

"You always leave the key in the ignition?" he asked.

"Yeah," she answered with a look on her face as if it were a ridiculous question. "Keep your head up. If that guy is still around, he'll hear us leaving," Kathleen said.

Chase nodded and pulled the shotgun closer as she put the Jeep in gear and pulled out, following a dirt road away from the property into the woods. As they cleared the property, the thick woods made it difficult to see very far. After a few miles, the trees thinned. The sun was high overhead, and the sky was still clear. It had warmed up nicely, and the smells of the forest permeated the air.

Chase looked out the window, taking in the scenery. "Man, it's beautiful out here. I can see why you left everything behind and came up here."

"Are you a city boy?" she asked.

"I grew up in Boston. My family never did outside stuff like camping or fishing. I mean, we played sports and stuff, but going to the woods to spend the night or going and cutting down a real live Christmas tree never even seemed like a thing to do. Is that weird?"

"I think it's normal for city kids," she said. "I grew up in a bunch of different mid-size towns, and camping and fishing were pretty normal. That's probably why when I had the chance to live out here, I couldn't resist. It was almost like I was supposed to be here. I didn't realize how much I missed the mountains until I got here."

The dirt road was rough and narrow, and it was covered with a blanket of snow about two or three inches thick. Kathleen followed the tracks that looked as if a car or truck had come and gone a few times. Kathleen was careful as she maneuvered their way down the hillside.

Mountains hugged one side of the road, and a steep cliff was on the other. Chase wondered what would happen if another vehicle came from the other direction. There wasn't a turnout. Someone would have to back up until the road widened enough for them to pass each other, or one would have to pull off to the side and let the other go by.

Kathleen suddenly slammed on the brakes as they came around a bend. Chase caught the shotgun before it tumbled to the floor.

The Jeep slid to a stop, and they both looked out the windshield at two tremendously large, downed trees blocking their path.

"Damn," Chase said picking up the shotgun.

"Think it's a coincidence?" she asked.

"Nope, Look at the trunks. They've been freshly cut. Someone purposely blocked the road. How much further do we have to go to get to the store?"

"I'd say about five or six miles."

The trees were large. Kathleen figured the bumper of the Jeep would come to almost the center mass of the round trees. She asked, "Do you think I can push them off the road with the Jeep?"

"No, but let's try, anyway. Light on the gas. We don't want to high center on them."

Chase got out and guided her. Kathleen pressed the front bumper to the first tree and slowly pressed the gas. The tree didn't budge. She gave it more power, and the tires spun, spitting snow and mud behind the Jeep.

Chase held one hand up for her to stop. "It's not going to move."

"Damn, looks like we are walking from here," she said.

"Keep your eyes open. We're not alone," he answered.

## CHAPTER
# FOURTEEN

Kathleen and Chase walked for a while. Traveling downhill in the slick snow and frozen sludge was almost as taxing as walking uphill. They got tired and breathed hard. They opted not to follow the road to avoid being sitting ducks for whoever blocked the road. They assumed they were being tracked. This meant maneuvering the downward slope off-road in the deeper snow, and it made for extremely slow travel.

Dark cloud cover developed, and the temperature dropped. Chase tried to pull the small jacket around him tighter. He put his hands in his pockets and shivered. He was unable to get warm without a shirt, and the still-damp pants added to his misery.

Without warning, snow fell from the sky. It was a light, easy dusting at first, but then, as if someone opened the spigot on a faucet, larger flakes filled the gray sky, creating a curtain in front of them. There was so much downfall that the ground was quickly blanketed with a fresh layer of snow on top of the previous frozen layer, causing them both to frequently slip. Visibility was reduced to just a few feet in front of them. It was hard to watch for threats.

Kathleen carefully walked just a few steps in front of Chase. They had walked a while, and she was getting tired. She lifted her right leg when the frozen ground beneath her gave way and she slipped and fell hard.

She landed violently on her butt. With momentum from the fall mixed with the fresh powder on top of the ice snow mix below it, she descended the hill at a furious, unstoppable pace.

The whole thing happened so fast that Chase didn't have time to react. She was quickly out of sight, and only then did he hear her scream.

He yelled for her, "Kathleen!"

Slipping and sliding down the hill like it was a water slide, she went end over end, side to side, tumbling in every direction as she descended further.

Chase fled after her as quickly as he could, following the path she left behind, but she slid too fast away from him.

The thick snowfall obscured his view, making it impossible to keep up. He trekked down the hill as fast as he could. Then, without warning, he lost his footing and landed hard on his back. He slid down the hill on the same path that Kathleen had left behind. This made his descent slicker and much, much faster than hers.

He tried to maneuver himself upright but couldn't. Snow flew into his face as he slid from side to side, tossing and turning. Realizing it was going to be impossible to stop, Chase submitted to the hill and allowed himself to ride the slope as if it were an Olympic winter sporting event.

At one point, Chase slid past a rather large black bear who lazily gave chase for a moment and then gave up. "Jeeezuuuusss!" he said to himself in disbelief.

Further down the hill, Kathleen struggled to see where she was sliding. She was afraid she might smack right into the trunk of a large tree and kill herself or at best get seriously injured. She used her elbows like ski poles, avoiding the use of her hands for fear of breaking a finger. Even through the numbness, she occasionally felt the sting of a rock or stick smacking her relentlessly. Tears streamed from her eyes and quickly froze to her face.

Suddenly Kathleen reached the bottom of the hill, sliding into what seemed like an open field or meadow. She tried to stop her momentum with her feet and hands, but she continued sliding. Even though her clothes were already wet from the snow slide, it felt like her backside was getting wetter, extreme wetness. Her eyes widened. *It must be the lake!* Suddenly, *crash!* The ice gave way and Kathleen fell into the icy water. *Worst possible scenario. Don't panic, don't panic!* she told herself.

Kathleen gasped for air as the freezing water stole her breath. She tried to pull herself out, but the ice was too slick, and her hands slipped back down over and over. She was exhausted. Her hands were so cold they shook uncontrollably. Then she felt herself being pulled from the opening in the ice by the water's current. She tried to claw at the ice opening with her fingernails, but her hands screamed at her in pain.

The current pulled her away from the opening in the ice. *It's the river, not the lake. Shit!*

Her energy was depleting because it was more and more difficult for her to stay in the opening. She tried again to pull herself out. It was no use. Her hands were freezing, and she was shaking uncontrollably. Her breath filled the air each time she exhaled, and her lungs felt like two boulders weighing her down.

Suddenly, it seemed like she might be making some progress. In a daze, time seemed to slow down. Everything moved at half speed. Half of her body was out of the opening. Her legs and waist remained in the water. "P-p-please," she said aloud.

She lifted a little more. She felt a smile behind her frozen lips when she recognized that she was almost out. "Almost ttttthere," she said through chattering teeth. Her wet body slipped on the ice, making it difficult for her to get the rest of her body out. "Just a little bit more."

At that moment, she believed she was going to get herself out. Suddenly, the ice under her hands and chest broke, and she fell back into the water. This time, she was completely submerged. The current grabbed her and pulled her away from the opening. Panic. *Oh my god!* She could see the top of the ice cover above her. There was no way out.

She rolled along underneath the frozen top, and she was able to strike the ice with her hand a couple of times, but the ice was too thick and didn't even crack. It became more difficult to hold her breath. She knew if she didn't get out of the water soon, even if she did find an opening, she would die from hypothermia or she would drown.

Her vision blurred, and she could no longer discern which way was up. Slowly, her world faded to black, and she floated away with the current.

Chase slid to the bottom of the hill, following Kathleen's path. The snowfall had decreased somewhat, so his vision was slightly improved, and he realized that he was sliding on ice, which caused concern.

Ahead, he saw the opening in the ice, and he slid right toward it. *Oh, my god! She's fallen in!* He kicked at the ice with his heels, attempting to stop his slide. He didn't want to fall into the freezing ice water again.

A large piece of the ice that once covered the opening had lodged into the ice sideways. He rolled over to his side. He grabbed at the wedged piece of ice with both arms and tightly wrapped himself around it. Got it! He stopped inches from the opening. He laid flat all sprawled out attempting to spread his weight out over the ice as much as possible. He listened for cracking. Nothing.

He cautiously got to his feet and yelled, "Kathleen!" No answer.

He inched to the edge of the opening as close as he dared. She wasn't there. "Damn!" Through the opening, he could see the direction the current was traveling. He got down on his knees and used his arms to clear the snow from the top of the ice, so he could see through it. He didn't see her, but he crawled around searching for her until he got close to the riverbank. Once on solid ice, he stood and scanned in a complete circle, looking for Kathleen.

*There!* Closer to the edge, he could see what looked like a shadow moving under the ice. The shadow was hardly moving, but it was moving enough for him to notice.

As he staggered in that direction, he slipped and fell right on his face. His chin hit the ice, and he bit his tongue. Following the extreme pain, the taste of copper filled his mouth. He heard a crackling, and the ice broke. He fell into the freezing water.

The cold took his breath away as he tried not to panic. *Shit! Not again!* he thought. He kicked his feet and felt the ground underneath. Realizing he was in the shallows, he stood up. He swiftly broke his way through the ice toward Kathleen, spitting blood as he went.

When he got to her shadow, he broke the thin sheet of ice that was over her, and he pulled her out. He dragged her to the edge and laid her down on the snowy bank. She was blue and not breathing. He felt for a pulse. Nothing. He started CPR. Thirty compressions, one breath, over and over, not giving up.

"Come on, Kathleen!" he yelled.

More compressions and breath.

Finally, her eyelids shuttered. Her chest rose, and she coughed. Water spit from her mouth, and Chase rolled her on her side. More water escaped. She was trying to talk. They were both shivering from the cold.

"What did you say?" he asked.

"I..I...I...I'm freez...freezing," she said with a hoarse voice.

"Stay awake!"

Chase picked up Kathleen and carried her away from the water into the woods. He not only needed to find shelter but needed to find cover. There was still at least one bad guy out there somewhere.

He worked his way back toward the hill they had just slid down. He scanned the bottom of the hill parallel to the river. He struggled to keep going. Just as he was about to panic, he spotted a small shanty 100 yards away. He once had heard about some small hunting or fishing structures that are often found in the woods. They're not a cabin but just a small, loosely constructed shelter that hunters or fishermen used when they are out during the season.

Chase stumbled to the door with Kathleen in his arms. He kept reminding her to stay awake. *Damn!* It was padlocked. He set Kathleen down and kicked the door, hard with one foot. It easily flew open, leaving the padlock and hinges behind on the door frame. He picked Kathleen back up and went inside. He kicked the door shut behind them with the heel of one foot.

The shelter was more like a four-walled, one-room shack; it was barely bigger than an ice fishing structure, but it had a wood stove with a gray tea kettle on top and a counter area for preparing food, probably for fresh fish or game. There were two wooden chairs by the stove and what looked like an old Army cot in the corner. He laid Kathleen on the cot. Her eyes were closed. "Kathleen! Wake up, Kathleen." She didn't answer, but she was breathing.

After putting Kathleen down, he felt a surge of fatigue hit him. The adrenaline rush from falling into the water, finding Kathleen, performing CPR, and then carrying her all the way here, made him work up a sweat.

Now that things had settled down, he became very aware that his clothes were completely drenched. His hands were turning purple. Ice had formed on his brow and his breath was visible. *Soaked, again!* He thought.

He worked quickly. He spotted a large ax and split firewood stacked in neat a pile by the stove and flipped the wood stove door open, filling it with the smallest of pieces. There was a small pile of newspaper on the floor, and he shoved it under the wood.

"Shit! Matches!"

He went to the counter area and franticly went through the shelves. "Where are they?" His hands were numb.

He looked back, behind a can of Folgers instant coffee, next to a box of shotgun shells, he spotted a box of stick-matches. He grabbed it and raced back to the stove. He clumsily struck a match on the side. The paper lit quickly, and the smaller pieces caught fire. He filled the stove with some of the larger pieces and left the door open.

He warmed his hands. They tingled painfully as they thawed. Then, he scooted Kathleen, cot and all, closer to the stove. On the other side of the shack, he saw a pile of green wool military-style blankets. He quickly stripped Kathleen of her soaking clothes. He then went over and grabbed two of the green blankets and covered Kathleen. He took the tea kettle off the top of the stove and ran outside. He clutched handfuls of snow and stuffed it inside the kettle until it was full. He returned it to the stove.

The fire was blazing, and it didn't take long for the small shack to warm up. Chase suddenly worried, *This fire is going to scream to anyone looking, here we are. Come get us.* He remembered the box of shotgun shells.

Suddenly Kathleen coughed, pulling him from his thoughts. He went back to the shelves and found a spool of string. He strung the string between two nails in the walls near the stove. He pulled his boots off and set them next to the stove. He pulled the wet wool socks off, dropping them to the floor with a slosh. Kathleen's eyes were still closed, so he unbuttoned his pants and took them off and he removed the much too small coat. He then hung all the wet items, including her wet clothing, on the string to dry.

He grabbed the last remaining blanket and wrapped it around himself just as the tea kettle began to whistle. He went to the table and scooped two spoons of instant coffee into his cup and filled it with water from the kettle. He took a sip and pulled back quickly, "Damn!"

The liquid stung the sore on his tongue. He blew into the cup and took a more careful sip, attempting to miss the sore area in his mouth.

He took a moment to scan the room for anything he could use for a weapon. He walked over and picked up the ax next to the woodpile. *Better than nothing.* The ax was somewhere between a mini-ax and a machete. It had a large ax head, thinner than a regular ax, that was painted red, and the handle was half the length of a regular ax.

He placed the ax on the floor near Kathleen.

He was somewhat relieved to have the ax since they had lost Kathleen's handgun and shotgun when they slid down the hill.

He knelt in front of the stove and loaded more wood, glancing at Kathleen. Her eyes were open slightly, and she was silently watching him.

She asked in a raspy voice. "Where are we?"

"A little shack I found by the base of the hill we slid down."

"My chest hurts," she said, placing her hands in front of her over the blanket. "Last thing I remember is falling through the ice. I was underwater and couldn't find a way out. It was so cold."

"I pulled you out of the water. You weren't breathing."

"You gave me CPR?"

"Yes."

"You saved my life?"

Chase smiled, "Well, I guess we're even."

Kathleen lifted the front of the blanket covering her, "Where are my clothes?"

He pointed to the clothesline behind her. She leaned her head back, surveying the clothesline.

"You were soaking wet," he said sheepishly.

"You fell in the water, too?"

"Yeah."

"Again?" she asked, teasing him.

He shrugged and pulled the blanket tightly around him.

"In the time I've known you, you've been naked more than you've been dressed."

He responded with a smile. "And we haven't even been on our first date yet."

# CHAPTER
# SIXTEEN



John Simon was concerned. As he pondered his next move, he nervously tapped his fingers on his desk. He hadn't heard from Chase in over twenty-four hours. He made it very clear that he wanted Chase to check in every day. *Should I give him more time?*

Despite being a royal pain in the ass, Chase was usually dependable and followed instructions. He decided that he had to assume things did not go as planned.

Frustrated, he pulled out his personal cell phone and called an old friend, Sergeant Jerome Crawford, who worked for the Idaho State Police. He didn't want to give Crawford too much information but just enough to make his request a priority.

When Crawford answered, they exchanged pleasantries, and then Simon explained that he had a former associate that lived in a cabin up there and he hadn't been able to reach her. He was simply requesting a welfare check. Simon asked Crawford to either call him back or have Kathleen contact him once he made contact. Crawford told him that he was more than happy to help an old friend.

## THE WHITE HOUSE - CHIEF OF STAFF'S OFFICE

"Damn it!" Chief of Staff Harrison yelled into the phone. He had just been informed that Kathleen Wood and the unknown male slipped away and were on the run.

"How the hell did that happen? I thought you took care of that guy?" he asked.

"He got away," the voice on the other end said.

"Good Lord! Of all the incompetent sons-a-bitches!"

"Sir."

"Don't sir me. Stand down. I'm coming to you. Do you hear me? Don't do another thing until I arrive!"

"Yes, sir."

As he disconnected the line, he let out three consecutive "F" bombs.

He dialed a new number. He told the person on the other end, "I need a chopper, ASAP." After a pause, he continued. "I can't use Air Force Two for this. It's off-the-books. No one can know. Can you make it happen or not?"

He listened. "No, I don't want to be picked up on the White House lawn! I'll drive to the helipad."

He listened. "Very good. One more thing. I need three or four trustworthy, able to keep their mouths shut, former military freelancers for security. This must be on the down low. They will be paid very well to accompany me. I'll also need two private security Tahoe's with four each on the ground in northern Idaho ready to roll when I arrive."

He listened and then said, "I want to make it very clear. Once we're finished, I need to trust that they will forget everything that happened."

He listened. "I've already tried to let other people handle it! They lit the side of a mountain on fire! In the snow for Christ's sake! Don't tell me what I already know and don't lecture me. We're friends but not that good of friends."

He listened more, then said, "Listen, I'm about to announce my running for President of the United States. I need to make sure this gets done properly, once and for all. And I need it taken care of now. I'm announcing my candidacy next week. When this is over, David Patterson and Kathleen Wood will wish they had minded their own business."

He listened. "Your concern is noted. Wheels up in one hour. I want to be in Idaho by evening."

He hung up and pressed the intercom button on his phone.

"Yes, sir." Jessica's voice sounded upbeat.

"Cancel the remainder of my calendar today and tomorrow. I have a situation out of town I need to take care of."

"Okay?" she curiously answered as if waiting for more information.

He let go of the button, hanging up without responding with more details. He knew Jessica was fishing, but *damn it, she works for me. She knows what I want her to know, nothing more.*

He opened the bottom drawer of his desk and grabbed a bottle of aspirin. He twisted the top, shook out three pills, and popped them in his mouth. *This is gonna be a long day.* He tossed the bottle back into the drawer and slammed it shut.

C hase made Kathleen a cup of instant coffee. They had spent the last few hours listening to the crackling wood in the stove. While she napped on and off, he paced, keeping an eye out for threats.

Chase sat in the chair by the wood stove and set the ax beside him. Kathleen opened her eyes to Chase smiling at her.

"So, what does 'The Hamptons in Iraq' mean?" he asked handing her the cup.

"I think the less you know the better," she answered, sipping from the cup.

"C'mon, Kathleen. My life is in danger, too. Simon told me that you might be in danger, but I didn't expect this. I know your friend David Patterson is involved. He said something that he shouldn't have and now..."

"Wait. What? Did you say David? David Patterson?" she asked.

"Yeah. Patterson, I think."

"Simon said David was involved in this, too?" Her mind was spinning. She hadn't spoken to David in years.

She finally said, "If all of this is about The Hamptons in Iraq, I don't know who to trust."

"Really? Are you implying that you don't know if you can trust me or Simon? After all that's happened, if Simon wanted you dead, why would I pull you from the water, give you CPR, and make sure you didn't freeze to death? I could have just let you float away under the ice."

Kathleen paused in thought; *that makes sense.* She weighed her choices and finally said, "There was this palace in Baghdad that belonged to Saddam Hussein before the Iraq War. After we liberated Baghdad, many American forces' command staff set up residences in some of Saddam's palaces. American VIPs, like congressmen, senators, and businessmen with monetary stakes in the effort would stay there, along with military command staff.

"The American Government started sending millions of dollars, and I'm talking about actual cash flown into Iraq and transported by truck on pallets wrapped in plastic to the palaces and other places. The money was supposed to be used to pay tribal leaders for information and security, but there was no accounting. None. No one could say definitively where all the money was going. Even today, no one really knows where all the money ended up. Friend or foe, no one knows."

"That doesn't surprise me," Chase told her.

"Well, some of us started getting suspicious when these VIPs were leaving with far more luggage than they arrived with. You know what I mean?"

"That doesn't surprise me either."

"We started keeping a log of comings and goings."

"We? You and David?" Chase asked.

"And our friend, Greg. We kept a log of dates, times, and names and started taking pictures. I'm talking about some very powerful people here." Kathleen paused as if she was unsure if she should continue. She watched Chase's face to see if he was following.

"Ok? So, what did you do?" Chase pressed for more.

"I sent an encrypted copy of all our data on a thumb drive to Simon, and I mailed another copy to my P.O. Box in the States. Once I got back to the States, I transferred it to a safe deposit box.

About a month after sending it to Simon, I got an ambiguous email from him saying something to the effect of, 'Wouldn't it be nice to set foot on American soil again? Some never make it back. I trust you will carefully consider the high stakes and ramifications if anyone were to find out what you have done. It's not safe or smart. This is not a game Kathleen. Tread carefully.'"

"Ok? And?" Chase asked.

"I assumed he was telling me to let it go," she said.

"That's what it sounds like to me. But, let me guess, you didn't."

"I did. I haven't even picked that thumb drive up since I put it in the safe deposit box."

Chase asked, "Do you think Simon was on the take, too?"

"I never saw him skimming cash or anything else for that matter. He might have known what was going on and chose to keep a blind eye, but he would never compromise his integrity like that. Honestly, I don't think he has a crooked bone in his body. He might look the other way to stay in the game, but as far as I know, he's clean. He recruited me."

"Then what happened?" Chase asked.

"Greg, David, and I continued to take turns logging and photographing who was coming and going."

"Why?" Chase asked. "What good would it do to have that?"

"Now, when I think about it, I don't know. But back then we thought we could get it to someone and blow the corruption wide open. What we didn't know was how wide the corruption was. We each took turns watching. Each morning, the three of us would meet in my quarters and update each other on any new arrivals and departures.

"One morning, after Greg's shift, he didn't show up. David and I waited for about an hour before deciding to try to find him. When we arrived at his quarters, there were MPs outside his door. They told us that Greg committed suicide. I looked through the doorway and saw some men bagging up all of Greg's belongings." Kathleen recounted emotionally.

"I'm sorry."

"I just couldn't believe that Greg would commit suicide. I still don't. Anyway, shortly after that, I retired and returned to the States. I decided to go off-the-grid. I got the cabin and have been fine until now."

"Well, Simon must know something. That's why he sent me to you. We need to get back to Virginia. And we need to get that thumb drive from your safe deposit box." Chase said.

Kathleen looked at Chase curiously. "It's safe."

Chase sipped the last of his coffee and stood up. "I'll warm some more water."

For a few more hours, they made small talk and Kathleen began feeling better.

After finishing his second cup, Chase walked to the counter and set the cup down. He glanced out the window. He did a double take when he caught a movement in the trees. He turned to Kathleen with panic and opened his mouth to say something. Before he could speak, the window shattered, he flinched, and he fell to the floor.

"Chase!" Kathleen yelled. "Chase!"

Kathleen tumbled onto the floor and turned Chase over. He had vacant eyes and didn't appear to be breathing. There was blood on the side of his head near his temple, and a puddle of blood formed around the back of his head on the floor. Kathleen kept low. She wanted to continue to check Chase, but another shot flew through the window exiting through the wall on the other side. She knew she had to move. She reached for her clothes and quickly dressed. She pulled her boots on and crawled to the ax.

Another shot flew through the window and continued through the back wall. Another shot came. Then more in quick succession. There were so many shots into the tiny hut, sunshine bled through the numerous holes, making a Swiss cheese effect through the dusty air.

She stayed as low to the floor as she could, waiting for a pause so she could make a break for it. She gazed down at Chase again.

He hadn't moved. A lump developed in her throat, but she swallowed it back down. *Get your game face on Kath or you're going to be lying next to him.*

The volley of shots stopped. She listened and heard nothing. No more shots. No sounds of activity at all. She shimmied on her knees and elbows to the window with the ax in tow.

She waited. Listened. Still nothing.

She grabbed a pan from the counter and held it up in front of the window, expecting it to be flung from her grasp by a bullet, but nothing happened. She pulled herself up enough to look out the bottom corner of the window. Seeing no signs of a threat, she stood and leaned closer to the window's edge. Still no sound and no movement. It was as if the shooter had disappeared like a ghost.

She carefully walked to the mostly destroyed door, with the ax down by her side. She peered out slowly. A shot rang out, barely missing her, hitting the doorframe to her left. Instinctively, she stepped out, pulled the ax back and forcefully flung the ax toward the threat, and then ducked back into the shack.

She heard a deep grimace and then the sounds of someone running through the icy snow. *Get on offense. You're never going to get out of this playing defense all the time,* she thought as she peered out again. She saw footprints going toward the woods and followed.

She came to a wooded thicket where she found a lot of bullet casings mixed in the snow. The footprints led further into the woods, trailed by blood in the snow.

"Gotcha, you bastard," she whispered.

# CHAPTER
# EIGHTEEN

Kathleen tracked the footprints and blood in the snow for about one hundred yards. The blood puddles got thicker and deeper red with each yard she walked.

She came across an AR-15, lying on the ground next to her ax. Blood covered the blade. She picked up the AR and checked to see if there was a round in the chamber. There was. She pulled the magazine out and saw it was still half full. She hooked the strap over her shoulder and kept walking. The sporadic puddles of blood had turned into a snakelike, uninterrupted red trail, pooling in areas.

*He's losing a lot of blood,* she thought.

She continued onward, coming to the edge of a small ravine where the blood trail suddenly ended. She looked over the edge and saw nothing. Then she heard a movement to her right. She turned, dropped to one knee, and raised the newly acquired AR's sights to her eye in one smooth movement. With her finger on the trigger, she targeted a man who was sitting in the snow with his back resting against a tree. He was fifty-ish, heavyset, and wore a white camo-snow suit. His long salt and pepper hair fell from the hood to his shoulders. His breath was hard and raspy, escaping from lips framed by a well-groomed salt and pepper goatee. The snowsuit hood was pulled up over his head.

Blood flowed from his left side, puddling in the snow next to him. One entire side of the white snowsuit was red from his ribcage down to his shoes. Blood dripped from the side of his mouth. The man tried to lift his right hand, which held a Glock 9mm, but he didn't have the strength.

"Don't even think about it," Kathleen told him as she moved closer. She had him sighted at center mass and her index finger rested on the trigger.

"You're dying. Even if you could kill me right now, you'd never make it out of here alive. You've lost too much blood."

The man stared blankly at her without saying a word. He coughed and blood beads sprayed from his mouth, covering his goatee and the front of the white snowsuit. Kathleen leaned down and took the Glock from his weak hand. She strapped the AR-15 over her shoulder and pointed the Glock at the man. "So, do you want to tell me what the hell this is about?"

The man just looked at her.

"Tell me! Is it Harrison? Simon? Talk!"

His eyes glazed over. She shook his shoulder with her free hand. "Is this about Iraq?"

He looked right through her.

"Tell me! Is this about Iraq? Who sent you?" she yelled at him.

He didn't answer.

"Damn you! Who sent you to kill me?"

The glaze momentarily disappeared, and focus came back to his eyes. He locked his eyes on hers. His mouth opened, and he struggled to get his words out. He gave a weak chuckle and said, "He won't stop looking for you. He won't stop." He chuckled more as if he had just told an off-color joke.

"Who? Who!" she demanded.

He grimaced and then a large cloud of warm breath exhaled and floated in the air in front of them. He slumped over, and his face buried into the snow.

"Damn it!" she screamed.

A faint noise caught her attention, and she quickly knelt, aiming her gun in the direction of the sound. She crooked her head slightly, trying to make out the sound. It was faint but slowly got louder. Then she realized what it was.

Thump, thump, thump.

She felt panic rise in her throat. She quickly got up and found cover just in time to see a small black helicopter clear the corner of the ravine, flying low and heading in her direction. "Damn!"

She dashed past the dead man and the tree he had been leaning against. She sprinted about thirty yards to a tree line, getting behind the largest tree trunk she could find, and she stopped. She watched the helicopter continue up the ravine and crest the top. It was coming directly toward where the dead man now lay as if they knew exactly where to find him. It hovered just above him.

She saw the side door of the chopper slide open, and two men wearing all back fatigues jumped out. They raced to the dead man. She didn't dare fire at them. She didn't want to give away her position, and she knew that she was outgunned. She watched for any sign of who the men were.

They loaded Chase's murderer into the chopper.

Then the armed men walked back toward the bloody spot in the snow. She watched as one of the men indicated he saw her footprints leading to the tree line that she was currently hunkered down behind. They simultaneously raised their guns to their face and slowly began walking in her direction.

*I'm burned*, she thought.

Knowing she had to respond, she raised the AR-15 and fired a volley of shots at the men, hitting one in the leg. They backtracked to the helicopter, keeping their heads low. The uninjured man helped the injured man back inside the helicopter.

Once inside, they returned fire in Kathleen's direction through the door. Tree limbs splintered above her. She fired another quick volley of shots. Some shots ricocheted off the chopper's metal siding back into the woods. The pilot instinctively lifted the helicopter into the air.

Kathleen fired again, this time the volley of shots caused black smoke to billow from the back of the engine. Quickly the helicopter elevated and flew back in the direction it had come from, leaving a lingering smoke trail behind.

Kathleen didn't dare move, yet. She waited to see if the thumping sound vanished or if it would return. She didn't want to be out in the open if they circled back around. Checking her surroundings, she decided against working her way down the steep wooded area. Not hearing the chopper return, she slowly walked out of the thicket, passing where the man had been lying. All that was left was the imprint from his body and his blood in the snow. She decided to backtrack to the shack and regroup.

## LANGLEY, VIRGINIA – CIA HEADQUARTERS

John Simon was extremely worried. He had just hung up with Sergeant Crawford from the Idaho State Police.

Crawford said he hadn't had a chance to go up and check on Kathleen yet, but he just got dispatched to the market located at the bottom of the hill Kathleen's cabin was on. Clint, the owner, had dialed 911. Something about a helicopter and some men who just ransacked the store. It was hard to believe. Crawford asked dispatch if Clint sounded like he had been drinking.

"Negative, he sounded scared."

That was enough for Crawford, he was en route but wanted to call Simon and let him know about the call. He didn't know if it was related to Kathleen, but it seemed strange. Simon thanked his old friend and asked to be updated as soon as there was more information.

Black helicopters screamed *"Government."* He needed a backup plan for his backup plan. This is getting out of hand.

As Kathleen walked back to the shanty, her mind raced. Chase was dead; now there was a black helicopter with professional soldiers.

*Government? Freelancers? Something else? But why now? Who? None of this made sense.*

When she left Iraq, she put all of that behind her. Chase talked about Simon and David. She knew she had to try to find them since it was her only lead.

She wasn't completely sure she could trust Simon, but she desperately wanted to.

By the time she arrived back at the shanty, she had decided the priority was to get her copy of the thumb drive, contact David, and then figure out the next step. It occurred to her that if they were after her, they were probably after David, too. She decided she should try to warn him the first chance she got.

She slowly stepped into the bullet-ridden shack. She looked on the floor and gasped.

*NO BODY? Chase was gone!* There was blood on the floor, but no Chase.

Chills rushed down her spine. Confusion clouded her vision.

She quickly exited the shack and spent what seemed like hours backtracking to the Jeep. The entire way she tried to make sense of Chase's body being gone and what it meant.

When she finally reached her Jeep, she was surprised to see the log that had been blocking the road had been moved and was now resting on the roadside. The Jeep had been pushed to the side as well. She looked around and hoped it was some good Samaritan. She got in the Jeep, revved the engine, turned the heat to high, and sped down the hill toward the supply store.

After a short drive, she parked behind a medium-sized wood building. Out front, the sign read, "Woodland Supply Store and Post Office." It was a cross between sporting goods, food and groceries, a home, and a camping supply store. It was a real one-stop shop in the middle of nowhere, and it also served as the only post office around for those few who lived on the mountain and surrounding areas.

She killed the engine and stepped out. She left the AR-15 inside and stuffed the Glock in her waistband at the small of her back. She noted that all seemed quiet; not a soul in sight. It looked like a normal day at the supply store, not unlike a hundred other times she had been there. This time of year, it's mostly locals in the area. The tourist season was over for the year, and only a few hunting parties passed through.

She took the three steps up to the front porch and made her way to the entrance. As she opened the door her mouth dropped. The store was completely ransacked as if there had been a robbery and a struggle. She pulled the Glock from the small of her back, checking the aisles for Clint, the storekeeper.

Clint was a genuine mountain man, grown and raised in the area. He was in his early forties with longer black hair and a full beard, resembling Grizzly Adams. His parents owned the store and worked at it until they were well into their eighties. He took over after it became too much for them to keep up with. They both passed away a couple of years ago. Mom first and Dad less than a year later at age ninety-one.

Since moving to the cabin, Kathleen and Clint had become

good friends, slightly flirty but nothing more. On a couple of occasions when they were talking, it felt like Clint was going to ask her out but he never did.

Kathleen took a quick look over the rest of the store confirming Clint wasn't around. She went to the post office area and checked her box and found it empty. *Damn!* Her key was gone.

Kathleen had left the key to her safe deposit box in her mailbox here. She had asked Clint if it was all right if she kept it there for safekeeping. The store didn't have safety deposit boxes, but Clint said it would be safe in her mailbox. He had no interest in what the key went to, and he had never asked.

Kathleen went to the office behind the mailboxes. The door was open. It was ransacked as well. The desk was tossed over, and various papers covered the floor. She looked around the desk and looked through the scattered mess. *NO KEY!*

Knowing she would need some cash, Kathleen checked the old-fashioned register and grabbed what little cash was there, mentally promising to pay it back when things settled down. She ran back outside, got into the Jeep, and pulled it up to the gas pumps. While she filled the tank, she calculated the miles. She assumed David still lived in Maryland. She didn't have enough cash for that kind of trip, and she didn't want to use credit cards.

Right now, Boise would be her best option. Her copy of the video was on a thumb drive that she stashed in her safe deposit box in Boise. It also included some cash and IDs for safe travel. The problem was the key to the safe deposit box was now missing.

Kathleen's thoughts were interrupted by a noise behind her. She swung around and pointed the handgun. The sound came from a nearby storage shed. "Don't shoot, Kath," a familiar voice said.

"Clint?"

"Yeah, I'm coming out."

The door opened, and the large mountain man appeared, clutching a shotgun in his hands. Kathleen ran to him and gave him a strong hug. "Are you all right?"

"I'm fine. I was out here taking inventory when I heard a helicopter. It landed right over there! You know we don't see that kind of action up here, so I just hunkered down like a muskrat and watched to see what all the hubbub was about. Three men got out and went inside the store. By gum, had they not been carrying rifles, I would have shown them what-for when they started messing up the place. Then they hopped back into that chopper and flew off. I was hiding out here in case they came back. I did call 911, but you know how that goes. It could be hours before someone shows up."

She didn't want Clint to know she was involved. She smiled and deflected. "Who'd you piss off this week?"

"No idea."

"Keep that shotgun handy. I have to go," she said, turning.

"Kathleen," Clint said,

"Yeah?" She turned back toward him.

"Need this?" Clint held her key in his extended hand.

A big smile appeared on her exhausted face. "You're my hero," she said, taking the key from him, grasping his hand for a brief moment.

"I don't know what they thought they were looking for, but after they left, I looked for what might be missing. I found your key on the floor by the wall. It must have fallen out of your mailbox when they were messin' up the place, and they didn't see it. Nothing else was missing. Kath, are you in trouble?"

Kathleen didn't answer. She moved closer and planted a kiss on his right cheek and gave him a look that said, please don't make me answer that.

Clint blushed, sighed, and said, "Get that Jeep filled up and get out of here, darlin'. No tellin' if they're coming back or not."

"You're a sweet man. Can you do me a favor?"

"You know I will."

Kathleen took the ballpoint pen from his front shirt pocket. She grabbed his right hand and she wrote a phone number on his palm. "Call this number. His name is John Simon; tell him I'm in trouble. Tell him I'm on my way to Boise and to send help."

"I'm worried about letting you leave here alone," Clint said.

"I'll be fine. Just call Simon and tell him what I said, okay?"

"You bet."

Clint watched as his friend finished filling the tank. She placed the nozzle back in its carriage and drove away without looking back.

# CHAPTER
# TWENTY

## NORTH IDAHO MOUNTAINS – KATHLEEN'S PROPERTY

Sergeant Jerome Crawford of the Idaho State Police was on his radio, calling everyone he could think of to assist with whatever had happened. He arrived at the cabin that John Simon asked him to check on. After taking the report at Clint's supply store, now this. He struggled to understand what was going on. The only suspects were men dressed in black who flew away in a black helicopter. Quite frankly, if Crawford didn't know Clint so well, he would have thought the man was losing his marbles.

Crawford realized there was a problem when he noticed light smoke rising a few miles from Kathleen's cabin. He hoped it was a coincidence, but he knew better. He chastised himself, *I should have known, he's CIA for the love. Getting a call like that only means one thing. The shit is about to hit the fan.*

There wasn't much left of what used to be a cabin. It was unclear what caused the fire that burned it to the ground, but one thing was for certain, it wasn't an accident. He was no fire investigator, but even he could tell this cabin was lit on fire.

He walked the perimeter of the site, looking for any charred bodies but not finding any. That was a relief.

*So, not a homicide investigation, so far.*

There were numerous sets of footprints. Strangely, Sergeant Crawford didn't find any spent shells, but he was sure the holes in the burned wood and the shed were bullet holes.

There wasn't cell service, so Crawford returned to the cruiser and dialed Simon from his sat-phone.

"What did you find?" Simon asked answering the phone without even saying hello.

"Not good, my friend," Crawford told Simon what he saw at the scene.

Then Simon began asking for more favors.

Crawford listened. "You want to do what?"

Crawford listened more. "That's a big ask. How much time do I have?"

After a longer listen, Crawford said, "Assuming I can pull that off, we'll be ready. But I can't promise we can get it done, and the next time you call asking for a simple favor, I'm not answering."

## BOISE, IDAHO

Kathleen periodically pulled over at rest areas and watched the traffic, looking for signs of being followed. At one point, she stopped and grabbed a hamburger at a local burger joint. The food felt amazing in her empty stomach and made her sleepy. She pulled into a rest area, put a full-size sun visor in the front windshield, leaned her seat back, and restlessly slept.

When she woke, she was surprised to find that it was nearly seven the next morning.

Back on the road, she constantly checked her rearview mirror, but she never saw anything suspicious. She remained vigilant and still made it to Boise with just under an eighth of a tank of gas left.

Just outside of the downtown corridor, close to the Boise airport, she came to a small one-story brick building that mirrored extinct locally-owned banks from years ago. A welcoming sign on the building read, "Hometown Credit Union." It was a small member-owned establishment, but it was large enough to have safety deposit boxes.

Kathleen checked the time. It was just after nine. The bank had just opened. She parked and pulled down the visor to check herself in the vanity mirror. She was shocked to see how disheveled she looked. She grabbed some wipes from the glove box, wiped her face, and cleaned her hands. She did the best she could with her hair and stepped out. A gust of frigid air shot a noticeable shiver through her body as she walked to the front entrance.

She was feeling uneasy; she didn't dare bring a firearm with her into the bank for protection, but without it, she felt vulnerable. She hated that feeling.

The bank had a lot of glass windows, and the drive-up isles were away from the main entrance. Inside, the teller windows lined one side, while the administration and loan officers' desks and cubicles were on the other. TV screens on the walls featured the latest news headlines, stock market tickers, and the most current investment and loan interest rates. Security cameras policed the entire operation.

As she entered, she skipped the teller line and went to the small row of cubicles. She didn't try to avoid the cameras; she didn't want to appear overly suspicious. A smartly dressed man looked up from his computer monitor and greeted her with a smile. "May I help you, ma'am?"

"I just need access to my safe deposit box please," she told him.

"Sure, no problem. I can do that. The room is free right now," he said. The man politely asked for Kathleen's identification. He punched keys on his computer and looked up at her as if comparing her ID photo to their records. Satisfied, he stood up and asked her to follow him. They proceeded past the row of cubicles and to the back wall. The boxes were housed inside a small, secure room. The employee punched in a series of numbers on a keypad.

There was an unlocking sound, and he turned the doorknob, opening the door for Kathleen. She thanked him as she walked in, and he closed the door behind her.

Kathleen quickly found her box, number 2525. She set it on the small table against the opposite wall and lifted the lid.

Kathleen had stocked her box with her *go-bag*. It contained everything she might need if she had to move quickly. There were multiple passports with various names and origins. It also had blocks of cash from varying countries, hair color, and colored contacts. A can of pepper spray, a satellite phone, and tucked beneath it all she found a thumb drive right where she left it. She let out a sigh of relief. This was the original with all the Iraq data on it.

*I've got it. Now, how do I use it to my advantage? How do I calm this down?* she wondered.

She put some of the American currency inside her bag along with the pepper spray, satellite phone, and thumb drive. She put the box back in the wall, locked it, and quickly left the room.

The banker looked up from his desk as she passed.

She gave a quick nod and a slight smile as she passed and exited the building.

She quickly started her engine and drove out of the parking lot, expecting something to happen but not sure what. As she drove down the road, she checked her rearview mirror. Everything appeared normal.

*Am I really in the clear with no one following me?* she wondered half amazed. "Seems too easy, doesn't it? Yes, it does," she said aloud.

Without a plan from here, she drove to the airport and followed the signs directing to long-term parking, unsure of what her next step should be.

She picked a parking level toward the top that was sparsely occupied and backed in so she could see if anyone else came up. She took out the satellite phone. She only had two names in her contacts. David and Simon. David or Simon? Chase said Simon sent him to warn her, and David had something to do with whatever was going on. She worried that David might be compromised, so she decided to risk calling Simon.

Just as she was about to press the call button, she detected movement in her peripheral vision. A man walked in her direction. She reached for the 9mm. The man was dressed in dark clothing and had a winter scarf wrapped around his neck and up over his mouth and chin.

She didn't panic; after the last twenty-four hours, she was past that. She was in the zone and all her military training and experience quickly returned. With the satellite phone in one hand and the handgun in the other, she wasn't concerned, just curious. She considered that this person could just be walking through the parking lot.

She pulled the gun closer and slowed her breathing, then the man pulled the scarf down, revealing his face.

*Could it be… David? Yes! It was David! But, how?* Her thoughts raced as she watched him quickly close the distance between them.

A wave of mixed emotions rushed through her. She was relieved, angered, curious, happy, rageful, irritated, joyful, and mad! The emotional conflicts bombarded her mind.

David raised his hand in a sheepish wave. He reached for the vehicle's passenger door and tried to open it. It was locked. He bent down to the window and looked in at Kathleen.

Bewilderment spread across her face.

He rapped on the window with one knuckle.

Kathleen was pulled from her trance. She stared back at him. For a split second, she hesitated to put the 9mm down but decided to trust her instinct. She pushed the unlock button.

David opened the door and got into the passenger seat next to her.

Kathleen blurted, "David, what the hell—?"

"Drive, Kath. Drive!" he told her.

"David! I don't—"

"Drive. We're not safe here. I promise I will tell you everything.

Just drive!"

She stowed the phone behind her seat, set the Glock next to her right thigh, put the vehicle in gear, and slammed her foot onto the gas. They quickly exited the garage.

She breathed heavily, asking, "What are you doing here? Last I knew you were in Maryland."

"Get on the interstate and drive toward Salt Lake," he instructed.

Small white snowflakes stuck to the windshield as she took the interstate on-ramp heading east. The faster she drove the more congested the view through the windshield got. She turned the wipers on, took her eyes off the road for a quick second, looking at her old friend.

"Damn it! Tell me what's going on!" Kathleen shouted. "You have no idea what I've been through!"

David yelled, "I did something stupid, Kath!"

"What? What did you do?" she pressed.

"This is all my fault."

"What's your fault?"

"This! And what happened at your cabin," he replied.

"How do you know what happened at the cabin?"

"Simon told me."

"Simon? You're in contact with Simon?"

"Yes. He said that he sent someone to find you at your cabin and bring you back to D.C., but he thought something must have gone wrong when he lost contact with whomever he sent. Then he got a call from someone he knew at the State Police who told him that your cabin looked like a war zone. Then he got another call from some storekeeper who said you told him to call Simon and have him send help."

"Clint called Simon, Okay. Good. What's going on, David? Why are they coming after me and who are they?" she asked.

"Damn it! I'm so stupid!" he said, hitting the side of the door with a fist.

"David! Tell me what you did!"

Kathleen was doing eighty when she slammed on the brakes and swiftly pulled to the side of the freeway. She put the vehicle in park and turned her body toward David, "All right! Out with it. Right now!"

Traffic whisked by, causing the vehicle to lightly wabble with each passing.

David sighed deeply and said, "The surveillance pictures and videos that we took in Iraq…"

"I assumed that had something to do with it, and?" she asked.

"Harrison," David said.

"Harrison? Yes, I remember him being in Iraq. He was top brass of that private security force, or maybe the CIA. He was skimming cash though, right?"

"Yeah."

"Okay? David, quit making me work so hard. Just tell me what you did."

"You know Harrison is the president's chief of staff now, right?"

"No. Chief of staff? I've been off-the-grid, and I stopped watching the news a while ago."

"Well, Harrison's been the chief of staff for the last two years. I heard a few months ago that he's considering a run at the White House himself. He's started an exploratory committee and is already raising money from big donors. Apparently, the president is encouraging him to do it since he's had his two terms, and there's never been any love between the president and the V.P. They hate each other."

Kathleen nodded, and David continued. "I had one of my contacts at The State Department get me Harrison's personal email address..." he paused.

"And?" Kathleen pressed.

"I threatened him," David whispered.

"How?" she asked a few decibels louder than before. "Threatened him, how?"

"I blackmailed him, Kath."

"How so?"

"I sent him one of the videos we had of him skimming cash in Iraq."

"Shit, David! And?" She pinched the bridge of her nose, closed her eyes, and sat back in her seat.

"I told him that a video like this could wreck a presidential campaign, and it would be a shame if one of the media networks got an anonymous copy. Perhaps he should reconsider his run for president."

"Wow! That was pretty dumb. You put a target square in the middle of your back. What does this have to do with me? How am I a target?"

David looked down at the floor. Traffic continued to rush by.

"David, what aren't you telling me?" she pressed, drilling her eyes into his.

He swallowed hard. "I told you everything. I don't know why they came after you for sure. I told them that *we* had multiple copies and that if anything happened to me, there were instructions for the videos to be sent to all the major news outlets. I guess for that to happen, I had to have help."

"Jesus, David! So, they assumed I was in on this with you because we were close in Iraq?"

"I guess. It wouldn't have been hard to figure out who I was close to. Aside from Greg, you were my only friend. Everyone knew how upset we were when he died. A few days ago, I'd gone to the corner market, and as I rounded the corner on the way back to my building, I spotted a white van across the street. You know, it was an obvious CIA ops van. I pulled up the house cam on my phone, and I saw guys rummaging through my apartment. I'm sure they were looking for the masters. I turned and walked the other way and haven't been back to the apartment since. I got in contact with Simon and told him what was going on. He was pissed. Anyway, he put me up in a safe house and said he was going to send someone to make sure you were safe. Then he got a call from his guy at the State Police who said that it looked like a nuclear bomb had gone off at your cabin, so he sent me to try to find you. I got lucky. When I spotted you at the bank, I followed you to the parking garage."

"How did you know I had an account at that bank?"

"Simon told me. I don't know how he knew. Anyway, we figured if you left the cabin, you would probably head to the bank. He knew you had a safe deposit box somewhere, and we assumed your go-bag was probably in there too. It was a logical long shot that paid off."

She felt a lump in her throat develop, and she tried to push it back down. She hadn't let her emotions surface much about Chase's death and everything that had happened. It rushed into her all at once.

She wondered again about what happened to Chase's body. She assumed Harrison's men cleaned up as they went. A single tear traced down her left cheek. She swallowed hard, checked the traffic behind her, signaled, and pulled back out onto the freeway.

## WASHINGTON, D.C., THE WHITE HOUSE

Chief of Staff Harrison was back behind his desk in the White House. After almost crashing in the helicopter in Idaho and missing the target, he decided it was best for him to be as far away from the area as possible, in case the media or local law enforcement started digging too deep. He couldn't afford to be seen in the area, so he returned to D.C. and waited for updates.

His phone rang. Seeing the contact's name, he answered with a scowl, "That's twice! Damn it! Find her! And where the hell is David Paterson?"

He listened. "I pay you to find people who can't be found, you moron! Do your job!"

He slammed the cracked phone down on his oversized desk again. This time, he caused a large piece of the glass screen to chip out, landing on the desk in front of him.

He was already irritated that Kathleen had gotten away from them on the mountain. He didn't expect her to fire on the chopper. They were fortunate when they discovered she had a bank account in Boise. They had contacted the bank manager, who agreed to let Harrison know if she arrived. The plan was to take her once she left the bank. But she had already been there and left before his men could arrive. They were combing the area, but she could be anywhere at this point.

On top of that, David was still unaccounted for. No one had seen him since the day Harrison's freelancers tossed his apartment.

Harrison was having a bad couple of weeks. He wondered if that boy scout Simon might be helping David. He knew he had to proceed carefully if that was the case. Going after Kathleen and David is one thing. But Simon? That would be a whole other story.

Harrison suspected if Simon knew what was going on, the CIA would have already paid him a visit. So, for now, they stay the course. He could deal with Simon when and if the time comes. He picked up the piece of glass that fell from the phone and tossed it in the garbage.

# CHAPTER
# TWENTY-TWO



Kathleen and David had just passed Ogden, and they left I15 for I84 heading east. They were roughly thirty-one hours' driving time from Virginia. They had been driving in silence for quite some time. Kathleen processed everything David had told her, and she wanted to calm down before speaking. David gave her time to do so.

After they passed South Weber and headed into the mountains, she finally said, "The man Simon sent to find me is dead."

Kathleen noticed David turn his head to face her.

She then said, "His name was Chase. He saved my life, and they killed him."

"I'm sorry, Kath. I never expected this to go so wrong." David told her.

"He got killed, David, protecting me. Because of what you did."

David sat in silence as the words stung him.

"So, we can trust Simon?" she asked.

"Yes," he answered.

"How did you get to Boise?"

"I flew. Simon got me on a flight under an assumed name, no questions asked."

"What was your exit strategy?"

"I didn't have one yet. Finding you was the priority. Just to get you somewhere safe while we figure things out."

"Figure things out? David, you can't blackmail someone like Harrison and think he's going to just do what you want and forget about it."

"I know. It was a spur-of-the-moment kind of thing. I hadn't thought it through, I guess."

"That's an understatement," Kathleen said. Reaching behind her seat, she got the sat-phone. She set it in David's lap. "I think it's time to call Simon. We're a long way from D.C., and I'm not sure that's the best place for us right now, anyway. We need his help."

## NORTH IDAHO MOUNTAINS

Sergeant Jerome Crawford of the Idaho State Police was amazed. When he called his old friend John Simon and told him what he found at Kathleen's cabin site, the CIA bigwig told him to secure the site with as few people as possible. Simon wanted the knowledge exposure of this incident limited to *need-to-know* or less. Simon said he was going to send his own cleanup crew.

Crawford did as he was asked and cleared all but the necessary security personnel, posting them on the perimeter and keeping everyone out. His job was to make sure the scene wasn't contaminated.

When three green military-size choppers landed just over the ridge, it was like the beginning of something out of a movie.

A dozen or so men trailed their way to the perimeter. The apparent leader, named Stanton, introduced himself and told him that they decided to save time and fly the supplies and personnel due to the rugged terrain.

Without hesitation, the men crossed into the scene and began the cleanup. Stanton told Crawford thanks, but they preferred to have the scene themselves and that the perimeter security team could clear it as well.

Crawford did as he was requested. He dismissed all the locals. He was the only local left on the mountain and watched from a distance, keeping out of the way.

## LANGLEY, VIRGINIA – CIA HEADQUARTERS

John Simon's satellite phone rang. Very few people had his number, so he hoped it was who he thought it was. The screen confirmed his hopes, and he answered, "Kathy!"

David answered, "John, it's David. You're on speaker, and Kath is here with me."

"I'm here, John," she said focusing on the road.

"Thank God. Are you all right?"

"I'm a little frazzled, but at the moment, we're both all right."

"Okay," Simon said with relief.

"John, Chase is dead." Kathleen choked back a sob.

"Damn it."

There was silence for a beat as all three seemed lost in their own thoughts.

"Kathy, I assume David has told you what this is about."

Kathleen glanced at David, then back to the road, "Yes."

"I've had to keep this quiet. I didn't want it to get back to Harrison that we're in contact. Sending Chase was a risk I had to take, but that didn't pay off, unfortunately."

"Especially for him," Kathleen said. "Harrison's men hit my cabin. He saved my life. We owe it to him to finish this."

"Agreed. So, involving the smallest possible circle of people, my only option was to send David, hoping you would show up at the bank. But, if I could find your account records, Harrison probably has as well. Where are you now?" Simon asked.

"Just outside of Weber, Utah," David answered.

"That's a long way from here," Simon said.

"Can't you send one of your CIA choppers to pick us up some-where?" David asked.

"I'm trying not to attract attention. I've already got three fully manned birds over at Kathy's cabin site doing cleanup. I worry about too much military air traffic attracting attention."

"John, while they're up there, have them clean up a shack in the wooded area to the south. It's where Chase was shot. His body was gone when I went back."

"Okay. So, it appears Harrison is doing some cleaning as he goes, too," Simon said.

"They tore up the little mercantile at the base of the hill. It would be nice to help clean that up, too," Kathleen told Simon.

"No problem. You're talking about Clint's place; the guy you had call me?"

She continued, "Yeah."

"I'll take care of it." Simon's desk phone buzzed, "Hold on guys."

Simon answered. They overheard Simon telling his assistant that he would take a waiting call through. Addressing David and Kathleen, Simon said, "You guys aren't going to believe this. Keep quiet. I'm going to put it on speaker."

Simon's desk phone buzzed again. He pushed the speaker button, "Hello, Sammy. What do I owe this pleasure?" Simon asked Chief of Staff Samuel Harrison.

Kathleen's eyes widened. She looked at David whose mouth had dropped open.

David silently mouthed to Kathleen, "Holy, shit!"

# TWENTY-THREE

Kathleen and David listened quietly; both seemingly held their breaths while they listened to the conversation between John Simon and Samuel Harrison. Simon at CIA Headquarters and Harrison at the White House.

"I'm well, John. I know it's short notice, but I was wondering if you might be free for dinner tonight. Say six?" Harrison asked.

"Let me look." Simon didn't look. He didn't need to; he knew his evening was completely clear.

After a long moment, Simon finally responded, "Could we do six-thirty? I have a prior engagement that might not end soon enough for me to make it at six." Simon waited for an answer.

There was a moment of silence. Everyone waited for Harrison, knowing he wasn't used to being asked to make accommodations. As the president's chief of staff, most people worked their calendars around his. Not Simon. He asked for an extra half-hour to mess with Harrison's ego.

Harrison finally answered, "That would be fine."

"What's the agenda? Do I need to have anything prepared?"

"We just haven't had a chance to see each other in a while. I thought it was about time." Harrison lied.

"You're not going to ask me for a political contribution or

endorsement, are you? You know I don't take sides on political races, and I strive to be non-partisan." Simon tried to knock Harrison back a beat.

"I haven't announced anything regarding my future, and I wouldn't dream of putting you in a position like that, my old friend. This is just a social call." Harrison lied again.

"All right. How about Marcel's on Pennsylvania Ave.?" Simon asked.

"Perfect."

"I'll make the reservation. See you tonight," Simon disconnected the call.

"The line is clear," Simon announced to Kathleen and David.

"Holy shit!" Kathleen repeated David's whisper at full volume.

"What's he up to?" David asked.

"He's fishing. He wants to know if I'm aware of what's going on and or involved."

"I don't like you meeting with him by yourself," Kathleen said with concern.

"Don't you worry about me. Political hacks like Harrison typically don't like to get their hands dirty. I'm quite sure this is just his way of fishing for information, and he wants to see my face as he casts his line.

"What do you want us to do?" Kathleen asked.

"I want you to stop at the next town and get some rest. Depending on how dinner goes with Harrison, I think I have an idea but you two are going to need to be sharp and rested. Find an out-of-the-way shithole that takes cash. I'll call you after my dinner."

## THE WHITE HOUSE – CHIEF OF STAFF'S OFFICE

Samuel Harrison got up from his desk and walked to the small table by the only window in his office. It was getting late. He gazed out. *What a view*, he thought, loosening his tie and exhaling deeply.

From his office, he could see Lafayette Square, and he had an unobstructed view of the Jackson Statue in Lafayette Park. It was the one with Andrew Jackson on horseback, raising his hat in one hand as he sits atop his horse above a large cannon.

*I'm a good, man,* he reassured himself. *I make a difference. This country needs men like me. Hell, this country needs me. I'm in the right place at the right time in history, right where I'm supposed to be. This is my destiny, and I won't let anyone take it away from me. Everything I do is for the good of the country. I'll do whatever it takes to get this little problem under control and, I will be President of the United States. Mark my words.*

He picked up a crystal tumbler from its upside-down position on a copper tray on the table. He opened the ice bucket and took out one large round ice sphere and put it in the glass. He poured a generous amount of Vodka into the glass over the ice. It was his favorite, Reyka from Iceland.

He squeezed a lime wedge into the liquid. He lifted the glass to his mouth and swallowed the entire helping in one gulp.

For the first time since all this started, he felt something gnawing at his subconscious. Something he wasn't used to or comfortable with. He felt his eyebrows crawl closer together as he tried to identify the unusual feeling. He gazed out the window until finally, it came to him. Worry.

He was worried about how this might end. Is it possible for the first time in his career, he might come out on the wrong side of things?

Alarmed at his own lack of self-confidence, he pushed the thought away and poured another drink of liquid confidence. He downed that one with one gulp as well.

# CHAPTER
# TWENTY-FOUR

## MARCEL'S RESTAURANT, WASHINGTON, D.C.

John Simon arrived early for his appointment at Marcel's. He wanted to make sure he arrived before Chief of Staff Harrison so he could catch him arriving.

Being early gave him the strategic advantage of choosing which seat to occupy. He preferred to sit with his back against the wall for a good view of the entrance.

Simon had already sent resources to Idaho with instructions to rebuild Kathleen's cabin. He directed the team to have the cabin area, wooded area, and Cliff's store all cleaned up as if nothing happened.

Jean-Pierre seated Simon at his usual table, a four-person table at the back of the room. Simon watched people come and go. Some he knew personally, and he waved or gave a quick nod to acknowledge them. Most patrons he either didn't know at all or he knew them and chose not to greet them, even if they attempted to make eye contact. He called it pot licking, and he hated pot licking.

In this town, it's more about whom you know and leveraging favors or pulling strings to raise your standing in the cesspool of

D.C. life-timers. Trump famously titled them "The Swamp." He felt this definition was spot on.

Say or think what you will about Trump, Simon often told people, he was right about one thing. The Swamp needed to be drained. Or, as Jack Nicholson once said in a *Batman* movie, "This town needs an enema."

Simon saw Jean-Pierre threading his way toward his table with Harrison in tow. Simon picked up his tumbler of Makers Mark Whiskey on the rocks and took a swallow. He and Jean-Pierre made eye contact. Jean-Pierre nodded as if to confirm his guest had arrived.

## GATEWAY INN, LYMAN, WYOMING

Kathleen and David found a rundown hotel just off Interstate 80 in Lyman, Wyoming, just as the sun set. They got one room with two queen-size beds. They paid cash and signed the registration as Mr. and Mrs. Iyam Nonya. David thought it was hilarious. Kathleen, not so much.

When they got in the room, David broke out laughing, "Don't you get it? Iyam Nonya, as in, I am non-ya, business?"

"I get it, David. Not very original," Kathleen said with an unimpressed tone as she collapsed down on the bed closest to the bathroom, giving David the bed closest to the window. She closed her eyes, suddenly realizing how tired she was. She nudged her way up the bed to a pillow. She pulled the fluffy cushion close and rested her head on it. She was fast asleep in less than a minute.

When Kathleen awoke, she heard the shower running from the bathroom. She stretched and rolled over on her side. She glanced at the clock and saw that she had been asleep for a couple of hours. It was about dinner time and her stomach told her eating soon would be ideal.

The door to the bathroom opened and David stepped out with a white towel wrapped around his waist. He pulled his wet hair back from his face. "Hey, sorry. I thought you were still sleeping." He grabbed his shirt off his bed and returned to the bathroom.

Kathleen didn't respond. She remained deep in thought, wondering what big idea Simon had come up with for them.

"Hurry up! I'm starving and there's no room service," she called out to David.

# CHAPTER
# TWENTY-FIVE

## NORTH IDAHO MOUNTAINS

Sergeant Jerome Crawford watched as helicopters came and went, some with supplies strapped to the bottom hugging the chopper with cargo netting. Men and women jumped in and out with supplies. In a matter of hours, Kathleen's cabin had been completely rebuilt. Crawford didn't know it, but the place was in better shape than the original.

The outside yard area was neatly landscaped with fresh sod that was soon to be covered in a light dusting of fresh snow. Raised beds that could be used for flowers or small vegetable gardens in the warmer weather were placed sporadically around the property. They were ready for the next spring.

Inside, the kitchen was rebuilt with new appliances, counter-tops, a sink, and a table. The living room had a new fireplace, a loveseat, and a new deep soaker tub that sat in the living room like before. It wasn't copper, but instead, it was pearl white with claw feet. Along one side of the tub, there was a plush white sheepskin rug.

The bedroom had a California king-size bed with thick quilts and large puffy pillows that took up most of the space, a modest size dresser, and a nightstand. Stanton thought Kathleen would find it comfortable when she got home.

Simon told Stanton to spend whatever was necessary on the fixup, which he did. He got the impression that Kathleen wasn't the extravagant type, so he took the liberty to make assumptions and didn't want her to be uncomfortable in her own home. They rebuilt the shop/barn and put up some decorative fencing around the perimeter. As a bonus, they installed motion sensors and a couple of cameras in the fencing for security. Later they would program the system and sync it to Kathleen's phone.

A similar operation was going on down at the bottom of the hill at Clint's supply store. Stanton's team told Clint that if he signed a non-disclosure and kept what happened to himself, they would clean up his place better than before. He signed without hesitation.

Crawford's team was also able to find the small shack where Chase was killed. They rebuilt or replaced the damaged areas and the floor where Chase's blood had stained the wood. It was obvious to anyone that looked that there were new boards placed sporadically around because they didn't match the well-weathered boards, but it was the best they could do in the allocated time. They were almost out of time and needed to get off the mountain.

## MARCEL'S RESTAURANT, WASHINGTON, D.C.

Simon played it cool as Jean-Pierre ushered Chief of Staff Harrison.

Simon half-smiled as Jean-Pierre announced his guests' arrival. "The other half of your party, sir."

"Thank you, J.P.," Simon said without standing. The gesture showed a lack of respect and screamed, "You don't intimidate me."

This didn't go unnoticed by Harrison. Jean-Pierre chuckled to himself at the snub and pulled a chair out for the new arrival. Harrison sat directly across the table from Simon. The battle lines had been drawn right down the middle of the table. Simon liked his odds. Ironically, so did Harrison.

"John," Harrison said, extending his hand out to Simon. "Good to see you, my old friend."

Simon extended his arm and accepted the handshake saying, "Likewise."

"May I bring drinks, gentlemen?" Jean-Pierre asked, motioning for a barmaid to join them. Harrison ordered an Old Fashioned.

Jean-Pierre held up menus.

Harrison declined the menus, telling him that there would be no dinner tonight, just drinks.

He nodded and left the men to converse.

Simon sat back, observing the man in front of him as if he were waiting for the serve at a tennis match. Whoever spoke first loses this volley. Most people are uncomfortable sitting in silence. Simon knew from years of interviews and interrogations that silence can be your friend and can make your opponent stumble while they attempt to break the uncomfortable silence.

Almost as if on cue, Harrison spoke, prompting a bright smile on Simon's face.

Harrison said, "I bet you're wondering why I wanted to see you tonight?"

"It crossed my mind. Policy?"

"No, my friend. I just wanted you to hear from me personally that I am planning on running for president in the next election."

Simon let out a snort as the other drinks were delivered. Simon said, "Well, thank you, but everyone in this town already knows that. If you were trying to keep it a secret, you have a major leak on staff you probably should address."

"I wasn't keeping it a secret. I just wanted to tell you personally."

"Why?" Simon quizzed.

"Because if I win the nomination of my party, then win the general election, I'm planning on nominating you for director of the CIA in my administration."

# TWENTY-SIX

David and Kathleen ate dinner at a small diner. The establishment prided itself on having a large menu.

Kathleen ordered a steak salad with herby vinaigrette dressing. David had chicken-fried steak with mashed potatoes and gravy and Brussels sprouts. Kathleen called it a heart-attack-inducing meal. David said he couldn't help himself. The food reminded him of when he was a kid growing up. His mother would make it for his father; it was one of his father's favorites.

They ate in silence for some time before Kathleen finally put her fork down and asked, "Why would you do that?"

"I've been asking myself that since the day I saw those guys in my apartment. It seemed like the right thing to do at the time. I just wasn't good with the possibility of Harrison becoming the president of the United States. He's as corrupt as they come. I wanted to stop his campaign before he even had a chance to get it started."

"C'mon, David. Most politicians are corrupt on one level or another. Think about it. How is it that so many politicians, Democrat and Republican, become millionaires after serving? Some even while serving. The whole damn system is rigged. So, why him?"

"I don't know. I guess I saw his corruption with my own eyes in Iraq. That cash was supposed to help rebuild, feed, and secure the country for its civilians. Harrison took it for himself as if he was owed it. The taxpayers deserve better than him."

"I don't disagree with that, but you know the power brokers in Washington, D.C. will do whatever it takes to keep their power. Look at Jeffrey Epstein, you really think he committed suicide in prison?"

David shook his head. Kathleen continued, "And now they're after us because they want Harrison in the White House."

"Who's they?"

"That's the question, isn't it?

## MARCEL'S RESTAURANT, WASHINGTON, D.C.

Simon lifted his glass to his lips and took a longer-than-normal sip of his drink. He took his time while he considered how to respond. He had been in this town long enough that almost nothing surprised him. Harrison was a savvy politician but offering Simon the CIA Director position surprised even him. It was such a blatant bribe.

Simon caught a twinkle in Harrison's eyes. He must have been pleased with himself.

Harrison seemed to be patiently waiting for Simon's response. Simon set his glass down on the table and decided to play along, knowing Harrison's offer was just a chess move, a bold distraction from the issue at hand. He knew Harrison had no intention of nominating him as director of the CIA.

Simon finally said, "I'm flattered, Sammy. I wasn't aware you followed my career close enough to consider me the right person for director."

"Of course, I have. There's not much going on in this town that I'm not aware of, my friend."

"I've heard that." Simon chuckled, trying to ease the tension.

Harrison smiled in response.

"If you don't mind me asking, why do you want to replace the current director? It seems to me Director Lee has things humming along quite well," Simon poked.

"Scott Lee?" Harrison asked with a supervised tone. "The man is a career bureaucrat, and sure, for the first time in a while the CIA isn't embroiled in scandals or controversy. The fact is, respect for the agency is still polling extremely low. I think someone like you could bring the agency back to life, back to being respected as the premier intelligence agency in the world. I would like to see it as an agency the public trusted, again."

Simon digested the comment a beat and didn't break eye contact. He finally nodded slightly and gave a non-committed response, "Well, it's still a long way to the general election. I wish you luck and should you win, I would be honored to revisit your proposal."

Harrison lifted his glass to toast the answer. He cleared his throat and said, "Um, and if you wouldn't mind, keep this close to the vest. Just between us, for now."

"Of course."

"Is there anything else I can help you with?" Simon asked.

They were still engaging in verbal volleying. Harrison's eyes squinted a bit as he tried to read Simon's face. "No, not today."

With that, Simon stood up. "It's been a pleasure."

Harrison also stood. They shook hands as Jean-Pierre approached and asked, "Leaving?"

Simon answered with a large grin, "I've got an early morning. My friend here will pick up the tab."

Simon gave Harrison a light pat on the back, and he walked out of the restaurant without looking back.

---

Harrison remained standing while he watched Simon exit. He picked up his drink and finished off what was left. Suddenly, he wasn't so sure Simon was still nibbling at the worm on the hook he cast. He looked at Jean-Pierre, "Check, please."

Harrison's phone rang. He pulled it from the front pocket of his blazer. He looked at the screen, recognized the caller, and put the phone to his ear, "I hope you have good news."

The caller told Harrison that they got a license plate number for the car Kathleen was driving from the video recording of the bank parking lot. He was then told that they gave the number to the highway patrol in the surrounding states and asked that it be entered into their roadside license plate readers. Just a few minutes ago they got a hit on the plate and were en route to intercept her in Wyoming.

A large grin covered Harrison's face. "That *is* good news. Keep me posted."

## GATEWAY INN, LYMAN, WYOMING

David awoke to the sound of the satellite phone ringing. He rolled over in bed and looked at the clock on the end table between his and Kathleen's beds. 6:22 a.m. *Good grief. It's too early*, he thought, wiping sleep from his eyes. The phone stopped ringing; he missed it.

He heard the shower running in the bathroom. Kathleen had her music on low. "Superstition" by Stevie Wonder played in the background. It was one of his favorite songs. He lay in bed with his eyes closed, sleepily bobbing his head as he grooved.

The water suddenly turned off and he heard the shower curtain being pulled open. The music stopped. He pulled the covers back and got out of bed. He pulled his pants on, grabbed his t-shirt off the nearest chair, and pulled it on.

After a few minutes, Kathleen came out dressed and looking ready for the day. David picked up the satellite phone off the nightstand. The missed call was from Simon. "Simon called," he told her.

"I'm starving, let's call him back from the car."

David nodded.

---

Harrison's men pulled into the parking lot of the Gateway Inn and stealthily parked across the street from the hotel, keeping eyes on the vehicle.

When the men saw David and Kathleen leave their room and get into the car, they followed for about ten minutes down the road until Kathleen and David pulled into a breakfast café.

The men pulled into a parking lot across the street from the greasy spoon and waited with rumbling tummies. The smell of hashbrowns and bacon filled the air.

"This sucks," one of them said to the others.

## LANGLEY, VIRGINIA – CIA HEADQUARTERS

Deputy Director Simon was at his desk, drinking his first coffee of the day. He had tried calling David and Kathleen but didn't get an answer. He wasn't too concerned. He assumed they were still sleeping.

There was a knock at his door and a woman dressed in a military Class-A uniform stepped in. Her blue blazer was adorned with gold buttons. Her blond hair was pulled back in a ponytail. She held a folder in her hands. She looked smart as a whip and capable of proving it.

Simon stood and greeted her. "Come in, Elizabeth."

She approached the front of his desk. Simon motioned for her to sit. She took one of the two leather chairs in front of his desk and set the folder in her lap.

Simon asked, "Looks like you found something?"

She nodded. "Are you sure you want to open this can of worms, sir?"

"Opening cans of worms is my specialty," he answered with a slight smirk.

"This file says Greg Kohl died in Iraq late in 1990. The strange thing is, there is no autopsy report in the file," she reported.

"Why is that strange?"

"I've never heard of an autopsy not being done under his reported circumstances of death."

"Really?" Simon responded with interest.

"Reads to me like someone wanted to close this case quickly and without scrutiny." She told him.

He held his hand out for the file, and she passed it to him. "No digital trace, correct? I don't want to chance Harrison putting an alert on the electronic file so he knows I'm looking into it."

"None, sir. This is the actual physical paper file, not a copy. It took a while to locate it, but it's all there."

He flipped it open and looked at Greg's military I.D. photograph attached to the front page. "Suicide or something more?" Simon asked rhetorically.

Elizabeth's eyebrows raised. "I feel the need to warn you. If this is what you think it is, you need to tread carefully. Samuel Harrison isn't someone to take lightly. More people have had their careers sidelined or have died suspiciously who were connected to him than the Clintons. And that's saying something."

"I'm not afraid of the Clintons, and I'm certainly not afraid of Samuel Harrison."

Simon continued reading then he looked up suddenly. "This says Kohl committed suicide in Iraq and his body was sent back to the United States shortly after, but it doesn't say who his body was released to or who his next of kin was. Is that normal?"

Elizabeth stood up. "I noticed that, too. No, it's not normal and that's where I stopped reading. His next of kin would certainly have been listed when he signed up. If you ask me, it's been scrubbed, or...?" she trailed off in thought.

"What? Or, what?" Simon pried.

"He was a mole. Maybe he never really had an official intake sheet done. Maybe he was there to inform the powers that be how the troops were doing or *what* they were doing."

"But why would they kill him?"

"Maybe they didn't. Maybe it was an extraction."

Simon's head shot up from glancing at the file. He didn't respond. He was in deep thought.

"And with that, I don't want to know any more about whatever you have stumbled into. I will say, please be careful. I kind of like you, and I would prefer you stick around for a while longer."

As she turned to leave, she looked back over her shoulder and said, "Oh, and remember, you didn't get that file from me."

"You were never here. Thanks, Ellie," Simon said with a smile.

Elizabeth left Simon to review the file. As he sat back in his seat, his sat-phone rang. David and Kathleen were calling him back. He picked up, "Hey, are you guys all right?"

"We're fine," David answered. "We just finished grabbing some breakfast."

"We're back on the interstate heading east," Kathleen said from the driver's seat. "John, it's a long drive from here to you. It could take us like thirty hours, and we don't have enough cash to pay for the fuel it's going to take to get there. I really don't feel comfortable using credit cards—"

Simon interrupted, "Kathy, get off at the next exit. Turn around and go back the way you came."

Kathleen asked, "Go back, to where?"

"I want you guys to go back to your cabin."

"Back to the cabin? There is no cabin. It burned down to the foundation, John."

"Don't worry about that, just get back there."

Kathleen and David were both silent.

"Oh, one more thing, I don't think Greg Kohl committed suicide," Simon flatly stated.

Simon heard tires screech.

"No shit!" Kathleen and David simultaneously yelled.

Kathleen nor David noticed a blacked-out Chevy Tahoe pass them when they suddenly stopped on the side of the road, but the occupants of the Tahoe certainly noticed them.

## CHAPTER
# TWENTY-EIGHT

Kathleen put the car in park and turned on the blinking yellow hazard lights.

David told Simon, "We were at his room the day he died."

"Did you ever see his body?"

David looked at Kathleen. They both searched their memories. Kathleen shook her head and David said, "No, we didn't."

"Kathleen asked Simon, "So do you think Harrison had him killed? And if he did, why didn't they come after us?"

"I said I didn't think Greg killed himself. I didn't say I believe him to be dead."

Kathleen and David looked at each other in disbelief.

"No way," David said. "Faking his death? Why would he do that? They tried to kill Kathleen. Greg would never go along with that. I don't believe it."

"Maybe you're right, maybe not. But here we are."

"But why would he fake his death?"

"I think, based on the irregularities in his personal file, that he was never an enlistee. I think he was a freelancing mole put in place to keep an eye on the troops. Once you three started your little surveillance op., they faked his death hoping to get you two to back off."

"And it worked, sort of," David added.

"Turn around and get back to the cabin. I have a plan," Simon ordered.

About a quarter of a mile past where Kathleen and David pulled to the side of the road, Harrison's men pulled off the interstate. They took the offramp and parked on a bridge that connected the on- and off-ramp to the highway. One of the men stood outside of the vehicle with binoculars held to his eyes. He wore black BDU pants, a black t-shirt with a "Punisher" logo on the front, a black flak jacket, black boots, and a black cap on his head. He watched Kathleen and David intently.

He could make out the two people inside the vehicle but could not see what they were doing. They could be possibly speaking to someone on the phone. He waited to see when they pulled back onto the highway. The plan was to sit tight, wait for them to get back on the highway and pass by, then pull back in behind them.

When the vehicle slowly pulled back onto the highway, he pounded on the roof of the Tahoe and told the occupants, "They're mobile. Get ready."

Just then, the vehicle he was watching quickly changed to the inside lane. Then, it pulled to the opposite shoulder and drove completely off the road and across the grass median, throwing dirt and gravel behind as it pulled onto the opposite side of the inter- state, traveling in the other direction, away from them.

"Damn it!" He opened the door, and yelled at the driver, "Other way! They're going the other way! Go to the other side! Go back the way we came!"

The driver of the Tahoe slammed his foot on the gas pedal, the tires squealed, and it lurched forward. He turned the vehicle around and drove toward the on-ramp to follow Kathleen and David who were now well out of sight.

The man with the binoculars pulled out his cell phone and hit a speed-dial contact.

After a few rings, Harrison answered, "Give me an update."

"Sir, they turned around and are now going back the way they came."

"Going back?

"Yes, west-bound. I'm not sure why. What do you want us to do?"

"Keep following. Not too close. Do not engage, just let me know where they stop."

"Copy that."

# TWENTY-NINE

eputy Director Simon was seated in a chair in the first row of a smaller agency jet. He requested a pilot, co-pilot, and one-person cabin crew. He specifically requested his regular crew member, Tiffany, if she was available.

Also, the co-pilot needed to be an agency drone pilot. This isn't unusual since many full-time agency pilots also have secondary duties. Many are exceptional drone pilots. He asked that the co-pilot bring his assigned mobile control unit with him and have the drone charged and ready to roll from its launching site.

It took him hours longer than he liked to get a green light for takeoff out of Washington, D.C., and he was relieved when they were finally airborne. He reserved the jet for three days. He hoped that he would have this whole dirty little distraction behind him within that time. He chartered the jet to Coeur d'Alene, Idaho airport where a private hanger had already been reserved. The jet would park out-of-sight, while he waited for Kathleen and David to arrive.

When they were about to start their descent, the co-pilot, who wore lieutenant stripes on his shoulders, sat across the aisle from Simon with an open laptop and headphones on his ears. His right hand expertly held onto what resembled a joystick for a video game console.

Simon held the sat-phone up to his ear.

David updated Simon on their location.

Simon told David, "We're starting our descent now."

---

Chief of Staff Harrison was also in a private jet. This one was not on the taxpayer's dime. Not that wasting taxpayer money ever concerned him. His motto is the old government saying, "Why buy one when you can have two at twice the price?" He always got a lot of laughs at parties when he said that joke as if he were being funny; he was serious. Two is better than one and it's always good to have a backup.

This flight needed to be kept quiet though. It needed to be kept off any official flight log, so he phoned up a friend, a very rich friend, and asked for its use. The friend, a Silicon Valley multimillionaire, wasn't using the jet at the time, and he gladly loaned it and a pilot to who he believed would be the next president of the United States. Nothing better than a major company CEO to be owed a favor from the president.

Harrison's flight didn't take off as early as Simon's so he still had a couple of hours of flight time remaining.

He spoke with his men who followed David and Kathleen, "I've sent another team to join you. They will tac up with you at the Lewiston exit. I'm done messing around. If the opportunity presents itself, just kill them."

---

After a smooth landing, the CIA jet taxied from the runway to the private hangar that had been reserved. The drone pilot turned the laptop screen toward Simon so he could see it. It was a live camera feed from his drone high above David and Kathleen; they were tracking them. They appeared to pass a small township or city.

Simon was still on the phone with David and Kathleen. He put one of his hands over the mouthpiece and asked the drone pilot, "Where is that?"

"They just passed Lewiston, sir. And, sir…," The pilot pointed to an area on the monitor, just behind David and Kathleen's vehicle. "An SUV appears to be following about a mile behind them. It's followed them as long as I've had them in my scope."

Simon took his hand off the phone mouthpiece, when the drone pilot said, "Look at that! Well, what do you know?"

Simon sat back up and looked at the screen again. The drone pilot held up two fingers.

"Two? Another vehicle?" he asked.

The pilot nodded.

"David, can you see anyone behind you?" Simon asked.

David answered. "I don't see anyone."

Kathleen said, "I've been watching this whole drive and haven't seen anything either."

"Well, since we've had you on a drone camera, we've spotted what looks like an SUV, maybe a Tahoe or Suburban, that's been trailing you the whole time. As you passed Lewiston, a second SUV joined in the chase," Simon told them.

Kathleen sarcastically said, "Well, it's nice to know we're not out here alone."

Simon responded, "We're guessing that each vehicle probably has four to five inside."

"That's not very fair," Kathleen said.

"My thoughts exactly. I'm working on it. I'll get back to you. Keep driving. Do not stop, and we will keep an eye on you."

"Copy that," David said.

Simon set the phone down on the table next to him.

The jet finished taxiing from the front of the airport to the far back side, into the secured private hangar. The large two-story tall doors were opened by men dressed like Secret Service or civilian security contractors.

Simon's regular cabin crew member, Tiffany, approached him and said, "He says he will be ready for you as soon as we come to a stop."

Simon asked, "Has he been waiting long?"

"No, only about fifteen minutes."

As the jet entered the hangar, it was directed to the right side of the hangar next to another jet. The parked jet was larger than Simon's. The stairs were already down and guarded by two men dressed in black suits with earpieces.

Simon rose from his seat. He straightened his tie, smoothed his clothes and hair, and told the drone pilot, "Keep an eye on them. If anything happens you call me right away."

The drone pilot nodded.

# CHAPTER
# THIRTY

Simon walked to the front of the jet. The pilot had already opened the cockpit door, Tiffany had the doorway of the jet opened and the stairs had been released ready for Simon to descend.

The jets were parked in such a way that each set of stairs matched where the other's stairs began, the last steps only a few feet from each other.

"Thanks, Jimmy. I won't be long."

"Yes, sir," the pilot answered.

"Play nice," Tiffany said with a smile as Simon descended his plane's stairs and took the three short steps to the other jet's stairs.

He stopped in front of the two security men in black suits.

The two men acknowledged Simon in unison, "Sir." Then one of the men said, "He's expecting you. Please go up."

Simon made the quick trek up the steps and was greeted at the top by a smartly dressed man wearing all white including white gloves who said, "Ah, Deputy Director Simon. So good to see you again. Right this way. He's expecting you."

The man stood to the side so Simon could enter the plane. As Simon passed, he continued, "I hope your flight was good. Ours was dreadful. This cold Idaho air is full of turbulence. Can I get you a beverage?"

"Flight was fine, Jasper. Thank you. Nothing to drink."

"Very well. This way."

As they walked into the cabin area, Jasper leaned close to Simon and whispered near his ear, "Watch yourself. He's in a dreadful mood. He's been barking into that phone the entire time he's been on the plane."

"Thanks for the heads-up, my friend," Simon said.

"Of course." Jasper smiled.

All the seats in the jet were empty. As they continued toward the back of the jet Simon eyed the silhouette of a man seated, on the left side of the club-style seating. As he approached, the man's mostly bald head was prominent, due to the man looking down.

United States Attorney General Nathaniel Calvin looked up. His reading glasses barely hung onto the tip of his nose. He scooted the spectacles back with one index finger. Then he held that finger up indicating that he needed one moment. Then he held the same finger to his lips, instructing Simon to be quiet.

The man was smaller in stature than by reputation. He had a slight crown of black and gray hair around the edge of his bald head, piercing green eyes, and he wore Navy blue khaki pants with a lighter blue button-up shirt, no tie, and a dark blue sport blazer.

The man's face turned red with anger. "I don't want any more shit from that ass hole! Don't call back until you have good news!" He set the phone down on the tray table in front of him.

"Sorry son-of-a-bitch!" he said more to himself, even though he was looking directly at Simon.

Jasper, who stood a step behind Simon, leaned in and said in a sing-song way, "See, I told you."

Simon smiled a large smile and said to the man, "I heard you were in a good mood today."

"Ha! You did not!" Calvin replied. "Jasper, I have told you not to talk about my moods behind my back?"

"I didn't tell him anything I wouldn't say to your face," Jasper countered.

Simon held his hand out and Calvin, who remained seated, reached out and shook Simon's with a strong grip. As he released Simon's hand, he looked past Simon and said to Jasper, "Well, how many times have I told you that leaking information about me could be a threat to National Security?"

"National Security my tush, you're just a grouch and I'll keep warning anyone you come into contact with Mr. Grumpy Britches," Jasper responded.

Calvin looked back at Simon and said, "See what I have to put up with?"

Simon chuckled and Jasper said, "You have to put up with? I've put up with you for almost ten years. I deserve the medal of honor or at least a raise."

"You just got a raise," The man told Jasper.

"That was before."

"Before what?"

"Before grumpy became your middle name. Your wife suggested you be nicer to people, remember?"

Calvin looked at Simon, shaking his head. "They team up on me all the time. Do you want something to drink?"

Jasper answered, "I already asked. He says he doesn't want a beverage. I'll bring you more coffee in a moment."

Jasper picked up the man's empty coffee cup from the tray, turned, and walked back toward the front of the jet.

Calvin motioned for Simon to take the seat across from him.

Calvin said, "Well, this is a mess. I went through all the information you sent over. I assume you have a plan. One that won't cause a political shit-storm like D.C. hasn't seen since..." He paused and then said, "Well, let's just say the country really doesn't have the stomach for another political scandal. Honestly, I have enough ulcers."

"I have a plan, but I need you to sign off on it. And I know Harrison is a friend—"

Calvin interrupted, "Friend, my ass! That egotistical, narcissistic bastard is lucky I haven't already had him arrested based on the information you provided."

"I think we can handle this effectively and quietly, without a scandal and a media circus. But we must keep the circle small, or it will leak. Trying to keep a secret in Washington, D.C. is nearly impossible."

"Who in your office knows?" Simon asked.

"Nobody.

"Good. My office is unaware too."

Jasper returned with a fresh cup of coffee for the attorney general. He set it in front of him and said, "I just got a text from Jessica. She said Harrison has borrowed a jet to get him here and then has a helicopter on standby to pick him up."

"Really?" Calvin asked.

"That's what she said. He doesn't know that she knows, but you know, if you want the scoop on what's going on in Washington, ask the assistants of the political leaders."

"Harrison is coming here?" Simon asked.

"Apparently," Calvin said.

"If Jessica says he's coming here, he's coming here," Jasper told them.

"I've got a new idea," said Simon.

As Simon returned to the cabin of his jet, he pointed to the drone pilot, "Where are they now?"

"North of Lewiston, sir," the drone pilot answered.

"More specific please," Simon requested.

"Highway 95, about an hour from Coeur d'Alene. Pretty much in the middle of nowhere."

"Are there still two vehicles following them?"

"Yes, but the second vehicle is trailing quite a way behind."

"How far?"

"About two miles."

"What's the traffic flow looking like?" Simon asked.

"Other than the three of them, the road is empty. Once they got passed the city of Worley, there hasn't been another vehicle on the highway at all in either direction."

"Perfect. Lock and load."

"Sir?"

"You heard me. I have approval directly from the attorney general himself."

"Yes, sir."

"And when this is all over. None of this ever happened. Understand?"

"Understood."

Simon sat in his seat and hit a speed-dial number on the satellite phone. A man answered on the other side. Simon said, "I'm going to need expedited clean up on Idaho Highway 95 a few clicks north of a city called Worley. How soon can you be there?"

Simon listened a beat and then said, "Get on it. We will be engaging momentarily. I need it done quickly and quietly. It never happened, understand?"

He disconnected and moved over to where he could see the drone pilot's computer monitor better and asked, "Show me."

The drone pilot pointed to a position on the screen. It showed, in real time the highway that the drone was flying high above. It was well out of eyesight of the targets far below. With his other hand, the drone pilot pressed a button on the controls. The frame zoomed into the target. He said, "Here are David and Kathleen."

Simon nodded.

The drone pilot pulled his sights off David and Kathleen and pointed the drone camera behind them. He said, "This is the first tailing vehicle. The one that's been trailing them the longest."

"Okay. How far would you say they are behind David and Kathleen?"

"Not all that far, a mile, maybe more."

Simon nodded. He could tell it was a black Tahoe or Suburban-type SUV. The drone pilot then moved off that vehicle and locked onto another vehicle quite a way behind the first trailing vehicle.

The drone Pilot said, "This is the new trailing vehicle, the one that joined them around Lewiston."

"Looks like a Tahoe or Suburban, too," Simon said.

The drone pilot made some adjustments to the controls and the camera zoomed in, close enough that they could read "TAHOE" on the side. Simon nodded as the drone pilot zoomed back out. He asked, "How far would you say that one is from the one in front of them?"

"I'd say about two miles. I'm not sure why they're staying so far back."

Simon said, "One vehicle behind you over a long period might make someone curious but two identical-looking vehicles following for a long time definitely looks suspicious."

Simon's satellite phone rang as the drone pilot said, "Makes sense. So, what do you want to do?"

Simon held up his index finger.

Simon listened to the man speaking on the other side and then said, "Just stay in a holding pattern. I'll let you know."

Simon asked the drone pilot, "Can you take the last vehicle out of commission without harming the passengers?"

"I can try, but I can't promise how the driver will respond upon impact. He could drive off the road and crash into a boulder and kill everyone inside or any number of other reactions that could cause the vehicle to crash. I have no control over that. But, if you're asking if I can make it so the vehicle can no longer operate, without blowing it to pieces, the answer is yes. This drone is equipped with laser-guided fifty-caliber rounds. I could target the tires. The vehicle will be undrivable after a hit like that, and if it doesn't crash, everyone inside will probably be fine, probably."

"Probably?" Simon questioned.

The pilot shrugged, confirming an element of danger.

"Understood, Lieutenant. Then that's exactly what I want you to do. Take that vehicle out of commission," Simon said.

"When?" the drone pilot asked.

"Right now."

"Copy that. Bringing my sensor operator online now."

Although the drone pilot was on the plane with Simon, this particular drone also required a sensor operator for laser-guided engagement. The sensor had been following the progress of this mission from an Army base in Colorado just in case they were needed. The drone pilot spoke into the mic attached to his headset, "Come in Romeo One."

Simon could hear the sensor operator respond through the drone pilot's laptop speaker, "Romeo One, I copy you ten-two."

The drone pilot covered the mic with the palm of his hand and told Simon, "That means, loud and clear."

Simon nodded with irritation, "Yes, Lieutenant. I'm aware."

The drone pilot spoke into the mic, "It's fourth down and we're going for it. I'm going hot and sending you the targeting information."

"Copy that. I'll be ready for the snap on your go."

"Stand by, Romeo One."

# CHAPTER
# THIRTY-TWO

Far above, in the northern Idaho sky, it was a beautiful fall day. The air was crisp, light blue, and cloudless. Mostly invisible to the naked eye, a twenty-million-dollar Army drone was getting ready to engage its target. This drone was called a Predator. It's light gray with a wide oval nose, over thirty-six feet in length, and twelve feet tall. It has a sixty-five-foot wingspan and a propeller on the end. It was an impressive and intimidating aircraft. For good reason, it was deadly and was ready to strike.

The target: a blacked-out Chevrolet Tahoe, traveling north on Highway 95 approximately a mile-and-a-half behind its sister vehicle. A total of five, assumed-to-be, heavily-armed hostiles occupied the target vehicle.

The current traveling speed was approximately fifty-two miles per hour.

The drone armed its laser-guided, fifty-caliber guns. The sensor operator laser-painted the lower backend of the Tahoe, near the wheelbase.

The drone pilot spoke into his mic to the sensor operator, "Romeo One, snapping the ball in, three-two-one- SNAP! SNAP! SNAP!"

Three rounds were fired. These bullets were called BMG and traveled around three-thousand feet per second.

Simon and the drone pilot watched intently from their vantage point in the airport hangar. Simon put his phone to his ear and said, "The ball was just snapped. You're clear to engage."

"Engaging," The man on the other side answered.

---

Harrison's men felt the intense impact, and the vehicle jerked forward. The rear wheels lifted slightly off the ground; both back tires blew out with loud bangs and the unsuspecting driver maneuvered, desperately attempting to keep the vehicle from running off the side of the road, crashing, or flipping over. The front airbags deployed slamming viciously into the front passengers causing whiplash.

"What the hell was that?" the driver yelled. He was blinded by the airbag and couldn't see out the windshield. He pulled out a knife from the sheath on his hip. He poked the airbag and pressed in forcefully to get the bag to deflate. With his other hand, he fought the steering wheel and applied the brakes. The Tahoe aggressively rocked from right to left. The front passenger pulled out his knife, deflating his airbag.

The backseat passengers were flung from side to side, brutally slamming into each other. Confused, they all instinctively pulled their 9mm pistols out of their side holsters and held them up, ready to face whatever threat was upon them.

This was supposed to be an easy payday with minimal resistance for these former special forces, now private contractor troops. It was sinking into all of them that perhaps the man who hired them withheld some vital information.

The man seated in the front passenger seat told the driver, "Get us to the side and stop this son-of-a-bitch before we take more rounds. If one hits the gas tank, we're screwed."

None of them could see out the windows. The deployment of the airbags released a film of white powder that had filled the cabin of the Tahoe and it stuck to the windows. With his sleeve, the front passenger used his arm to wipe the dusting off his window. As he wiped, through the side window he saw a large Blackhawk-type helicopter landing about fifty yards from them on the roadside. "Damn it!" he said out loud. "We're not prepared for a fight like this."

Then he ordered his men, "Holster your weapons!"

They all looked at him with confusion. "Now! Dammit! Before we all get killed. I don't know who the hell these guys are, but this is not what we signed up for. Holster!"

The men did as he instructed. The front passenger opened his door and slowly stepped out of the Tahoe onto the road with his hands held up. A half-dozen men had just jumped out of the side door of the helicopter, they all had their AK-47 long-gun sites on the man now standing in the road.

One of the helicopter men yelled, "Get on the ground! Get on the Ground!"

The man did as he was told and laid face down in the middle of the road next to the Tahoe with his hands on his head. As the helicopter men surrounded the Tahoe, the other doors opened, and the rest of the men exited and did the same as their leader, lying face down, hands on heads, on the roadway.

Their hands were quickly pulled down and zip-tied. They were escorted to the helicopter that was on the roadway in a holding pattern with rotors still spinning at top speed. This was to be a snatch-and-go.

After loading their cargo, the men got back into the helicopter, and it lifted off and flew back the way it came. The entire operation took less than five minutes.

As the helicopter slowly drifted out of sight a non-descript tow truck arrived. It was black with no name or company information listed. The two men in the tow truck took exactly two minutes to load the disabled Tahoe onto the bed of their truck, cover it with a thick green tarp, and drive away. Anyone passing this location would have no idea what just occurred.

The operation went exactly as Simon directed.

Back in the airport hangar, Simon clasped the drone pilot's shoulder. "Very good, Lieutenant. Thank you. We're done here."

The drone pilot spoke into his headset mic, "Romeo One. Touchdown. Thank you for your assistance and we'll see you at the prom. Over."

The sensor operator answered, "Save me a dance. Over and out."

# THIRTY-THREE

The helicopter carrying Chief of Staff Harrison hovered over the newly rebuilt cabin in the northern Idaho mountains near the Canadian border. He was taken aback, since last he heard the cabin had been destroyed, burned to the ground. After being told Kathleen was headed back to this location, he decided to take matters into his own hands and deal with it once and for all. *My daddy always said, if you want something done your way, you best do it yourself,* he thought to himself as he looked out the chopper window.

The chopper landed in the freshly laid sod several yards away from the cabin. As the chopper's sliding door opened, two men in full military gear jumped out and did a quick sweep of the location.

They returned and informed Harrison that the cabin was unoccupied and there wasn't anyone around. Harrison nodded. He took a Glock 9mm pistol out of its case, put it in his coat pocket, and hopped out of the chopper. The tails of his long coat flipped and flopped around him from the storm caused by the chopper rotors. He told the pilot to find a place to park out of sight where no one coming up the hill would see it.

Against their cautions, he ordered his two security guards to go with the chopper, leaving him alone at the location. As the chopper rose into the air, he walked slowly toward the cabin. It looked brand new. "Someone's helping her," he told himself. "So be it, I'll take care of them as well."

He took in a deep breath of the crisp, fresh air. *Wow*, he thought to himself. *If I could bottle this air, I'd make a fortune.*

Once inside the cabin, Harrison made his way to the kitchen. He found a tea kettle on the counter, filled it with water, and put it on the stove. He looked in the cupboard and found a box of instant coffee.

On Highway 95, neither David and Kathleen nor the men in the Tahoe following directly behind them, had any idea what had just occurred behind them. There was no sign that a second Tahoe ever existed. They were about ten miles from the turn-off that would take them to Cliff Woodland's Supply Store and Post Office.

The sat-phone rang, and David put it on speaker, "We're here."

"Do you see the vehicle behind you?" Simon asked.

Kathleen looked in the rearview mirror, and David looked in his side door mirror. Since they were on a straight stretch of highway, both could see the Tahoe about a half-mile behind. "We see it," she answered.

Simon continued, "Your turn-off is coming up. About a mile before your turn, the Tahoe won't be following you anymore. No matter what, just keep driving. I will meet you at the supply store. Do not continue to the cabin. Stop and wait for me."

"You do remember, there is no cabin left, right?" Kathleen asked.

"Just wait for me, Kath."

"Copy that."

The phone disconnected and she told David. "I guess that drone is still tracking us."

David turned the car radio up, mostly for a distraction. The Eagles' "Witchy Woman" played in the background. He looked into the sky through the side window.

# THIRTY-FOUR

Sergeant Jerome Crawford of the Idaho State Police was crouched behind a large boulder at the side of the highway near Kathleen and David's turn-off. He had a pair of spike strips lying on the ground next to him. Simon told him that the target was about a mile away. Crouching was not his strong point. At six-foot-two and two-hundred-fifteen pounds, it was not an easy task for the large man, especially with all his police gear on. The belt around his waist weighed around fifteen pounds and he had suffered from back pain for years. Crouching was not high on the list of things he liked to do.

The spike strips had short, two-inch hollowed-out metal spikes attached to a hard plastic frame that expanded upon release and retracted when pulled, like an expandable trellis. It was attached to a twenty-foot rope. Once deployed, and the strip is in place with the spikes up, the target vehicle would run over the spikes, and the rope would be yanked back by the officer, pulling the strip out of the way of any vehicles in pursuit.

Crawford had deployed spikes many times and felt comfortable in this situation. Although, success depended a lot on the driver of the target vehicle. If the driver spotted the spikes laying across the road, they could swerve or move off to the shoulder, which is dangerous. The driver could also lose control of the vehicle once the tires went flat and crash in an unexpected location. Either way, Crawford knew he needed to be vigilant and keep himself safe. He was taught in the Police Academy, "You can't help anyone if you get put out of the game. Personal safety comes first."

David and Kathleen traveled toward Crawford at sixty miles per hour with the blacked-out Tahoe still tailing them. As they came to a curve, they slowed to forty-five and maneuvered the elbow-shaped road. After the Tahoe maneuvered the curve, a State Trooper, under Crawford's command, pulled his vehicle into the middle of the road and turned on his overhead red and blue flashing lights. He planned to stop any oncoming traffic until Crawford told him it was clear to open it back up.

Over the radio, Crawford heard through his earpiece, "Target just passed, stopping all northbound traffic until all clear is given."

Crawford pushed the button on the side of his radio mic attached to his chest, "Copy that. Thanks, Mac." He got ready.

Deputy Director John Simon intently watched the drone feed. *A walk in the park,* he thought to himself. However, he still had an uneasy feeling since he had never worked with Trooper Crawford before. They met years ago at a law enforcement conference but, he didn't have firsthand knowledge of his skills. Although, training to deploy spike strips is a standard and not very difficult task.

Simon pushed Kathleen's satellite phone number and put the call on speaker. Tiffany brought him another cup of coffee and placed it on the tray in front of him. "Thanks, Tiffany. I think I could use something stronger at this point."

"Right away, sir."

Kathleen answered on her side, "Hey, I was getting worried."

"Everything is under control. We took out the second vehicle that was following you, so you just have the one behind you now."

David crooked his head around to look out the back window as Kathleen looked in the rearview mirror.

Simon said, "Keep looking ahead, David. I don't want them spooked."

David turned back around and looked at Kathleen, curiously. Then they leaned forward and looked up into the sky through the windshield.

Simon continued, "Now listen, coming up is another sharp elbow. Take it as fast as you're comfortable and don't slow down. There is a State Trooper on the shoulder with a set of spikes to deploy after you pass. We're going to take out the Tahoe behind you. You guys just keep driving. Don't stop. Get to Clint's place and wait for me there." The line disconnected.

David looked behind him to try and catch a glimpse of the Tahoe. Kathleen scolded with a smile, "Stop it, or Dad's gonna ground you."

<hr>

Simon continued to monitor the situation from his jet in the hangar. He hoped all the activity didn't get the media curious. One wrong word to one wrong person and this very covert operation could become a feeding frenzy, especially from the Washington, D.C. swampy press whose only allegiance is to the power vortex.

He often told himself, "The only ones I trust less than a Washington, D.C. journalist, is the Washington, D.C based CIA or FBI. Simon knew that for the most part, CIA and FBI field agents work hard to be non-political. But the closer the field office is to D.C. the more political decisions seem to be. Don't get him started on the press. In his eyes, there were no journalists left. There were only partisan reporters on both sides of the political spectrum.

Tiffany arrived with a tall glass filled with a red liquid and what looked like various pickled vegetables on an extra-long toothpick. She sat it down in front of him. Simon looked up curiously and asked, "You made me a Bloody Mary?"

"Yes." She set an additional napkin on the tray. "For any vegetables or olives, you don't want."

"I said I wanted a drink. Martini maybe?"

Tiffany stood up tall, "You didn't have lunch and you asked for a drink. I compromised. It's a drink like you asked, but it's also lunch. Enjoy your liquid lunch." With that, she smiled, turned on her heel, and walked away.

Simon picked up the glass, looking it over with a bit of a scowl on his face. He reluctantly took a drink. "Not bad," he said quietly, so Tiffany couldn't hear.

The drone pilot who had been watching this exchange chuckled.

"You stay out of this, mister."

"Yes, sir," the drone pilot answered. Simon took out a sprig of pickled asparagus from the glass and chewed it down.

The drone pilot pointed to his screen. Simon leaned over and saw that the target Tahoe was approaching the elbow in the road. "Here we go."

The Tahoe was about a quarter mile behind David and Kathleen. Kathleen took the elbow at fifty miles per hour even though the yellow caution sign suggested forty.

Crawford watched them pass. He quickly stood up with the spikes in hand. He forcefully tossed the plastic accordion of sharp spikes into the roadway. It expanded as he tossed. He held on to the rope, so it didn't get away from him.

It was a perfect toss, and the spike strip covered the entire lane and half of the lane running in the opposite direction.

———

Watching from the drone feed, a smile stretched across Simon's face. He took a big gulp from the liquid lunch Tiffany made him.

———

Holding on to the rope, Crawford scrambled backward to get out of sight. His shoe caught the side of the asphalt and he stumbled, almost falling, but he caught himself and quickly crouched back behind the boulder on the roadside. The pursuing Tahoe took the curve slower than Kathleen had.

As it came around the elbow to where the road straightened out, all four tires rolled across the spikes. First, the two front tires passed over the strip with a loud bang. More banging occurred when the two rear tires blew. The driver fought to keep the car on the road.

It was a perfect spike. Simon spoke into his satellite phone to men he had in a holding pattern, "You're free to engage."

As the Tahoe passed Crawford, he pulled the string with all his might, causing the entire spike strip to fling up into the air and out of the roadway. It flew over to the shoulder landing not far from him. He wrapped it up quickly and pushed it to the side as he stood watching to see what the Tahoe did next.

The spiked vehicle swerved from side to side intensely. During one swerve, the Tahoe banked to the right, causing the front and back left tires to lift off the road, then come crashing back down. The rubber from the back tire released completely from the rim and flew into the air. The rim hit the road sending sparks behind them.

The brake lights came on, as the driver attempted to maneuver it to the shoulder. Crawford heard a noise coming from overhead. He immediately knew a helicopter was approaching.

He watched the Tahoe slow to a crawl and gradually move toward the shoulder. He looked above to see a large Blackhawk-type helicopter landing about fifty yards away on the roadside.

A half-dozen men jumped out of the side door of the helicopter. All had their AK-47 long-gun sites pointed at the Tahoe, which was now at a standstill in the road. It didn't quite make it to the shoulder.

The helicopter men surrounded the vehicle. One man held up what looked like a tear gas grenade. He yelled, "Open the doors slowly and exit with your hands up or I'll smash the window and deploy tear gas."

There was no movement.

"Do it now!" The man yelled, "You have five seconds!"

Nothing. The man with the tear gas looked over at the next man on his right, "Cover me."

The cover man nodded, and the man with the tear gas took a step forward about to deploy the gas. Just then the front passenger door cracked. The tear gas man stepped back. He put the tear gas canister back in his flak jacket and lifted his AR-15 at the opening door.

Then, the other three doors opened slowly. The man yelled, "Exit slowly, hands in the air!"

In unison, all the Tahoe occupants slowly stepped out of the vehicle with their hands in the air. Once they were all out, standing in the road next to the Tahoe, another of the helicopter men yelled, "Get on the ground! Get on the Ground!"

The men did as they were told. Their hands were quickly zip-tied, and they were escorted to the helicopter, rotors still spinning at top speed in the road behind them.

The zip-tied men were loaded into the helicopter and the rest of the men got back into the helicopter. It lifted off and flew back the way it came, taking less than five minutes from start to finish.

Crawford watched, clearly impressed.

As the helicopter slowly drifted out of sight, a non-descript tow truck arrived. Two men took exactly two minutes to load the flat-tired Tahoe onto the bed of their truck, cover it with a thick green tarp, and drive away.

The only hint that anything had happened was a few deep grooves in the asphalt from the wheel rim of the Tahoe.

---

Simon was pleased as he watched from his vantage point. He picked up his ringing phone. It was the tear gas man from the chopper. "Ten total in custody. No injuries; they're quiet as a mouse. No one seems to wanna talk."

"Very good, you know what to do. I don't want them hurt, but one way or another, amnesia better set in, or we'll take another path. They need to forget this day ever happened. Make sure they understand."

"Copy that."

Simon hung up and took the last gulp from the Bloody Mary. He took the long toothpick out of the glass and ate a piece of pickled cauliflower and called to Tiffany, "One more, please."

Tiffany didn't answer, but she smiled.

Simon closed his eyes and let out a deep exhale. "Almost done."

He looked over at the drone pilot, "Let's get that thing over Kathleen's cabin."

Chief of Staff Harrison sat in a wooden chair next to the fireplace in the living room of Kathleen's cabin, sipping instant coffee. He was completely unfazed and unconcerned that he was breaking the law by being there and paid no mind to all the laws he had instructed his men to break since all of this started. Trespassing, breaking and entering, destruction of property, kidnapping, attempted murder, and murder.

It was simple in his mind. The ends justify the means, whatever the means might be. He had fully convinced himself that the actions he took benefited the country. He wasn't the only one skimming cash out of Iraq. If he went down, many other high-level government personnel could end up going down too. It would be a scandal with huge consequences.

He wasn't about to let this end his career, so this meant David and Kathleen needed to be silenced.

His personal cell phone rested in his lap. He didn't dare use his official government phone, knowing those pesky oversite committees like to comb through records, like a witch hunt.

*Oversite my ass. Overkill is more like it. Those politicians have no idea what it takes to keep this country safe,* he thought. *Sometimes rules must be bent. Sometimes we work in the gray. The world is not simply black and white. One-size-fits-all rules are ignorant and impossible to follow if the country is to operate at its highest level.*

He looked at his phone. The upper-right corner read, "No Service."

*Shouldn't be long now,* he thought. The last communication he had with his men was that they were about an hour out.

---

David and Kathleen slowly pulled up to the front of Cliff's store. As they stepped out of their vehicle, David shivered, there was a noticeable drop in temperature.

Cliff came out. He held a shotgun in one hand and a cell phone in the other.

David looked at Kathleen concerned.

"It's just me," Kathleen smiled at Cliff, holding her hands up as if surrendering.

A big smile crossed his face as he leaned the shotgun against the wall to his right. He slid his cell phone into his back pants pocket and held his arms open for a hug. "I'm so happy to see you, little lady."

He took the three steps down from the wraparound deck as Kathleen stepped forward and they embraced. "I'm glad to see you too, old man."

Cliff smiled and nodded his head toward David, who was still standing next to the vehicle. "Who's that?"

"A friend, David. David this is Cliff."

David walked over and the two men shook hands. "Come in, and I'll make us some coffee."

The three walked up the stairs. Cliff picked up the shotgun as they entered the mercantile. In the far-right corner, three medium-sized, four-person wooden tables were surrounded by chairs. "Take a load off. I'll grab some cups," Cliff said holding his hand out toward one of the tables.

"I know how you like your coffee, little lady. How about you, David? Black or with cream and sugar?"

"Could you do a latte by chance?" David asked.

Kathleen let out snort-laugh and Cliff shook his head unimpressed and said, "Not on your life, city boy."

"Cream and sugar are fine, thanks," David compromised.

Cliff gave Kathleen a devilish smile as he leaned the shotgun against the wall next to the table, and he left to grab their coffees.

Kathleen and David sat at one of the tables. David asked, "Do you trust this guy?"

"One hundred percent," she answered.

"He looks like Davy Crockett."

She chuckled.

David looked around the store that appeared to be caught in the past. A simpler time most thought long gone in America. "You lived out here?" he asked.

She nodded, "And loved every minute of it."

"That's amazing. It seems so… old-fashioned."

"There's more to life than fancy, overpriced coffee."

Cliff returned holding three blue enamel cups. He sat them down on the table in from of Kathleen and David. He then quickly retrieved a small container of sugar and two little plastic cups of cream.

"You've cleaned up nicely. Last time I was here the place was trashed," Kathleen said to Cliff.

"Can't take all the credit. A bunch of Feds showed up and insisted on helping get everything back in order and paid me for my time and losses," he told her.

"Really?" she asked.

He nodded.

"That's good." She sighed as if needing to confess. "Cliff, I borrowed some cash out of the register when I was last here. I promise I will pay you back when this is all over."

"Not a problem, darlin'." He smiled knowingly. After taking a sip of coffee, he continued, "Only catch was that I had to sign a non-disclosure and promise not to talk about what happened, ever. To anyone. Didn't matter to me. It's nobody's business. I don't even like people anyway. So, I signed."

Kathleen smiled, "Oh, you do too. Stop being that way."

Just then they heard vehicles pulling up out front. Cliff grabbed the shotgun and looked at Kathleen, "You expecting anyone?"

# THIRTY-SEVEN

The three stepped out of the front door of the mercantile; David and Kathleen trailing behind Cliff who had the shotgun. Cliff pushed the door open with his foot and held the shotgun up, the butt against his shoulder and the barrel lifted level to his eye.

There were two green, military-style Humvees parked near Kathleen's car. Four men in green fatigues were already out of one Hummer and the doors to the other were opening.

Upon seeing Cliff, the four men reacted in kind, lifting their AR-15 rifles toward Cliff, David, and Kathleen. "Drop the gun!" One of the men yelled at Cliff.

"You first, ass hole!" Cliff responded.

The four men quickly assumed a four-man, diamond formation, all targeting Cliff with their red-dot scopes. "You don't want to do this, buddy!" one of them shouted.

"Oh, I'm certain that I do, numb nuts. Try me. You're on my turf, rubber neck," Cliff responded."

You could tell the adrenaline was running high as the men's breath floated in front of them in the cold air.

Then three more men exited the other Hummer. They were

dressed like the first four, and each also targeted Cliff. Kathleen put one hand on Cliff's shoulder.

Cliff took his eye off the targets momentarily and looked at Kathleen.

The front passenger door of the second Hummer opened, and a person exited, but three men that surrounded the door were a protective blanket, and Kathleen, David, and Cliff couldn't make out who it was.

Two hands lifted above the three men's heads in a surrender posture, "Calm down everyone. I would hate for anyone to get shot. Careful. Careful, everybody."

Kathleen and David immediately recognized the voice. "It's Simon." She looked at David. "It's Simon."

David nodded.

"It's all right, Cliff. You can lower your gun. He's a friend."

Cliff looked at her with a cautious expression. Not lowering the long-gun.

Kathleen took a step forward and placed one of her hands mid-barrel on the shotgun, gently pressing it toward the floor. "It's okay."

Cliff gave in and lowered the gun.

Simon stepped around his men. He smiled, looking at Kathleen, "How nice to see you."

Simon instructed his men to set up a safety perimeter while he, Cliff, David, and Kathleen all went back inside.

Simon gave Kathleen a long, strong hug. "I'm so glad you're safe."

She smiled and they sat at a table. She then retrieved her copy of the Iraq, thumb drive and handed it to him.

He asked her, "Is this your only copy?"

She told him yes. Simon then looked at David. "When we get back to D.C., I want any and all copies you have too. Understand?"

David nodded.

Simon's cell phone rang. He picked it up and listened. They all watched Simon digest whatever he was hearing. They heard

Simon ask a few short questions, "Military or civilian? How many passengers? Would it be a problem? Can you do it out of public view? You're clear to engage."

Simon looked at the other three. "Our drone seems to have come upon a helicopter parked on the mountain about five miles from your cabin, Kathleen. Seems our predictable friend from the White House is out on a field trip, at your cabin."

"What cabin?" she asked.

Simon smiled with a twinkle in his eye.

———

The Blackhawk threaded its way through a ravine about twenty miles south of Kathleen's cabin. The intel from the drone pilot was that about five clicks north from their current position, a civilian helicopter was parked on a cliff. The rotors were not spinning, and it appeared to have a crew of three. A pilot and two probable private contractors for security.

The drone pilot saw the chopper drop Harrison at Kathleen's cabin then take off again and land on the adjacent ridge. It didn't appear to be equipped with guns and any resistance should be minimal. Their orders were to take it out of play.

Simon sent one of the Hummers and four of his men back to the Blackhawk to assist.

Once they arrived back at the chopper and got seated, a man inside gave a thumbs-up, indicating that they were good to go. The chopper lifted into the air.

After a beat, the chopper came around and got a visual of the target chopper parked on the cliff. Its blades spun as if it was about to lift off.

Snow flew around the chopper from the blade's powerful rotations. It looked like it was in a snow globe that had just been shaken.

"Shit! They're taking off!" the pilot told the rest of the team.

"Do not let that chopper get airborne!" the team leader yelled at the Blackhawk pilot.

The Blackhawk immediately went into a steep nosedive, rushing toward the helicopter. The target helicopter began to lift off the ground.

The Blackhawk accelerated and in seconds it was above the other helicopter.

The Blackhawk maneuvered sideways to the front of the other chopper. The pilots of both choppers were now face to face. The Blackhawk pilot raised his hand high so the other pilot could see clearly, and he motioned for him to land his craft with one finger pointing down.

The other pilot seemed to be looking around for an exit strategy. The Blackhawk pilot let loose one round from his fifty-caliber gun. He purposely drove the round into the clifftop directly in front of the other chopper.

Snow, ice, and dust flew into the air from the impact. The Blackhawk pilot motioned again for the other pilot to land. The other pilot didn't respond. He hovered in place, stalling, considering his options.

The Blackhawk pilot held up his hand for the other pilot to see. He signaled three different numbers with his fingers and then pointed to his headphones. The Blackhawk pilot then changed his radio frequency to the three numbers he just gave the other pilot.

"Come in, civilian aircraft," the Blackhawk pilot said into his mic.

"On channel," the other pilot answered.

"I am ordering you to land your aircraft. If you fail to comply, I have authorization to make you land by any means necessary. And I will not hesitate to fire upon you if you chose to ignore my warning."

Without answering over the radio, the other chopper slowly descended and rested on the clifftop.

"Civilian aircraft, cut your engine and tell everyone inside to get out and keep their hands up so we can see them."

The Blackhawk's side door opened, and two thick ropes dropped to the clifftop. Men in green fatigues descended. They had their AK-47 out in front of their bodies as they slid down, targeting the grounded chopper. Once on the ground, they took the pilot and crew into custody without resistance.

Chief of Staff Harrison heard the vehicle pull up outside Kathleen's cabin and he shivered as a chill of thrill ran up his spine in anticipation. He was surprised at the adrenaline rush that was overtaking his senses. It had been a long time since he had been out in the field. He felt like he did in his younger years working as an asset for the United States Government. He forgot how much he loved it. He took a deep breath and exhaled through his mouth, attempting to calm his blood pressure.

He remained seated at the table in the kitchen area, and although he had finished his cup of instant coffee quite a while ago, he never made a second cup. The sun was beginning to set, and from this vantage point, shadows draped across the walls.

He told the pilot of his helicopter to return at sunset, so he was glad Kathleen had finally arrived. Had she not, he would have had to leave for the night and return tomorrow. He felt working at night was a disadvantage.

He heard a car door open and then shut. His eyes widened with excitement. He licked his bottom lip with his tongue and then pressed his top and bottom lip together, wetting his whistle.

Harrison listened to the footfalls as they ascended the porch stairs toward the front door. He picked up his Glock 9mm pistol off the table and pointed it toward the front door.

He couldn't decide if he should shoot Kathleen as soon as the door opened and be done with it, or if he should let her come inside and explain to her why she had to die. Maybe if she begged for her life sincerely, he would let her live with the understanding that he owned her from this day forward. *Wouldn't that be something,* he thought as his arm lowered slightly.

Although it was too shadowed inside for him to see it, he could hear the doorknob slowly turning. He lifted the gun toward the door again. He decided that as the soon-to-be president of the United States, he wouldn't have time to *own* a former asset. *I'll just shoot her now, and David too, if he's with her, and be done with it once and for all.*

The door swung open, and Harrison fired three shots. Two shots flew directly through the open door, and one hit the frame splintering the new wood. He didn't see anyone at the door. He didn't hear anyone fall to the floor. Then, he felt the cold muzzle of a pistol being pushed hard against his head below his right ear.

He froze. His mind was scrambling.

A male voice behind him said, "Put the gun down slowly on the table in front of you."

Harrison opened his mouth, but before any words could come out the butt of the pistol smashed down on the back of his head, hard.

"Ouch! Jesus! Do you know who—"

A second strike came down even harder. "Put the gun down on the table in front of you, slowly," the man said again.

"Okay. Okay. Calm down." Harrison set the gun down. It was quickly retrieved by the man behind him.

There was a strange silence and no movement. Harrison felt the back of his head with his right hand. A large lump formed, and it felt wet. He looked at his fingers, *blood.*

He turned and looked behind him and didn't see anyone. He

didn't understand what was going on. He stood up when he heard footsteps approaching the front doorway. He froze.

He watched as the shadow first crested the doorway and then a man stepped through into the light.

"You son-of-a-bitch." Harrison said as he stood up.

"Sit down, Samuel," Simon told Harrison. He was holding a Glock pistol pointed at Harrison.

"You can go to hell, John! That bastard hit me on the back of the head! Twice! It hurt like hell." He rubbed the back of his head again.

"What bastard?" Simon asked.

"The asshole who hit me in the back of the head?"

"I'm not sure what you're talking about. I was waiting to make sure you didn't shoot out the door again. Now sit down," Simon said again.

When Harrison didn't budge, the man behind him stepped out of the shadows, he put a hand on each of Harrison's shoulders and forcefully pushed him down into the chair. "Hey! You're going to regret—"

A third blow to the back of the head. Simon pointed his gun toward the unexpected helper and yelled, "Damn it! Stop doing that! Who's there?"

The man stepped into the light. "Chase! Damn boy, where have you been?"

Simon noticed he had a white wrap around his head and there were some red splotches on his left temple. "Just trying to catch up."

Harrison looked confused and then put two and two together. He figured out that Chase must have been the man helping Kathleen when this whole thing started, "So, you must be the swimmer?"

"And you must be the asshole behind all this!" Chase returned.

Simon approached Harrison, "That's enough. Both of you."

Simon motioned for Chase to step away.

Chase objected, "This douche-bag tried to have me killed."

"I've got this. Take a step back." He motioned him to stand down by leaning his head to one side.

Reluctantly, Chase told Harrison, "Just give me a reason." Ashe slowly stepped aside.

Harrison asked Simon, "What the hell do you think you're doing here, John?"

"I could ask you the same thing," Simon answered.

"I, I, well, that's none of your business. It's classified," Harrison said.

"I have top-secret clearance, you egomaniacal…"

"Asshole," Chase finished Simon's sentence for him.

"I don't have to sit here and listen to you two. I'm the chief of staff to the president of the United States."

Simon scorned, "You know what I've noticed while working in Washington, D.C. all these years?"

Harrison didn't answer.

Simon continued, "Anytime someone gives their official title, it means one of three things."

"What's that?" Harrison asked.

"They're either trying to get laid, they're trying to impress someone, or they're trying to stay out of jail. Since I've never heard of you dating men, I'll assume it's one or both of the last two. I'm not impressed and keeping you out of jail is not high on my list of priorities."

"Why on earth would I be trying to stay out of jail?"

"Well, for starters your money skimming in Iraq."

Harrison scoffed.

"And more recently, you going after David Patterson, trying to kill Kathleen Wood, and your attempted murder of our friend there behind you."

Harrison said, "David Patterson was coming after me."

"And what did you do after he did that?" Simon asked.

"I didn't do anything you wouldn't have done in my position."

"You're wrong."

"No, I'm not. You enjoy the power you hold in Washington as

much as I do. John, put this all behind you and when I'm president, I'll make it worth your while."

Just then Simon and Harrison turned to someone entering the front door. "Sir, we're ready for you," Simon announced.

Harrison squinted his eyes trying to make out who was at the door. It took a minute but then he recognized the CIA director enter the cabin. Harrison stammered, "Scott? This isn't what it looks—"

The director held up his hand as if to say, stop talking. "That's Director Lee to you, sir. I heard you giving your title earlier, so I thought I would just point mine out as well. Since this appears to be a pissing match and all."

Harrison quizzically looked at Simon for help.

Simon shook his head and said, "You made this mess, Sammy. You went way over the line. You abused your position and power for personal gain. I wouldn't help you if I could."

Harrison looked at Simon and said, "You self-righteous son-of-a-bitch. You can't prove anything. Scott, I don't know what he told you but—"

Director Lee held up a small digital recorder in his hand and pressed play. It was a recording between Harrison and Simon that night at Marcel's restaurant,

Harrison: *"I bet you're wondering why I wanted to see you tonight."*

Simon: *"It crossed my mind. Policy?"*

Harrison: *"No, my friend. I just wanted you to hear from me personally that I am planning on running for president in the next election."*

Simon laughed: *"Well, thank you, but everyone in this town already knows that. If you were trying to keep it a secret, you have a major leak on staff you probably should address."*

Harrison: *"I wasn't keeping it a secret. I just wanted to tell you personally."*

Simon: *"Why?"*

Harrison: *"Because if I win the nomination of my party, then win the general election, I planning on nominating you for director of the CIA in my administration."*

Lee pressed the stop button.

Harrison told Director Lee, "That's not how it sounds. It's taken out of context."

Lee took out a satellite phone and pressed a contact. He walked closer to the table and put it on speaker. "Hello?" A voice on the other end answered.

Lee asked, "Are you ready for us?"

"I am. Stand by for the video feed."

Lee came closer and held the phone up, facing Harrison. It had a small screen that was fuzzy at first, but then it came alive. Harrison's eyes popped open wide when he saw who was on the other end, United States Attorney General, Nathaniel Calvin.

"Nathaniel, sssir?" Harrison looked at Simon and then Director Lee. He realized how much more serious this had just become. He asked the two men in the room, "What does the attorney general have to do with this?"

Attorney General Calvin said, "Mr. Harrison, you have the right to remain silent. I suggest you take it. I just wanted to show you some video so you will understand why you're about to be arrested.

The screen changed to the video recorded in Iraq from Kathleen's thumb drive. The video clearly showed Harrison packing handfuls of cash into a large suitcase. It appeared to be tens of thousands of dollars.

Then the video changed. This time it showed an interview room with one of the men arrested from the Tahoe that was following Kathleen and David. The sound came on. A man was mid-sentence. "... That's what your partner told us, too, but I need you to tell me who hired you."

The Tahoe man answered, "Chief of Staff Harrison."

"He hired you personally or hired the team through an intermediatory?"

"Well, he paid us through a shell corporation, but I spoke with him personally, as well."

"How much did you get paid?"

"We got half up front, $500,000. We haven't been paid the second half yet."

"Was lethal force authorized?"

"If necessary."

The screen went black. Then, the attorney general came back on the screen, and he said, "Chief of Staff Harrison, you are under arrest, and you will be arraigned in the morning. Scott, take care of our guest. Now, if you'll excuse me, I have to go have an uncomfortable conversation with the president."

"Yes, sir." The CIA director ended the phone call. "Let's go."

Harrison's chin quivered, "Scott, please. Is this necessary? I get it. You're right. I went too far. I'll cancel my campaign. I won't run for president."

Simon nodded to Chase who stood behind Harrison. Understanding his order, he lifted Harrison by his armpits, quickly pulled his wrists together behind him, and zip-tied them in the blink of an eye.

Chase led Harrison out the front door. As they descended the stairs, the back door to a green hummer opened. Kathleen stepped out. Her eyes expanded at the site of Chase. She squinted as if trying to focus. Recognition appeared, and her face glowed with a huge smile. Her eyes welled up with tears. She bolted to meet the two men.

She pushed past Harrison completely and focused entirely on Chase. She moved in close, pushing her body against his. She gently put a hand on each side of his face, pulled his head down, and kissed him hard on the lips.

Harrison hmphed.

She slowly pulled her lips from his just enough to whisper. "Where have you been?"

"Looking for you," Chase answered.

"What is this the love boat?" Harrison bellowed.

Kathleen released Chase and looked directly at Harrison. Her unblinking eyes were cold. A long moment passed until Harrison finally dropped his gaze and laughed to himself. "You know, you're a real bitch."

"And you're a piece of shit. You're lucky I let Simon handle this. I wanted to take you into those woods and spill your blood in the snow."

Harrison rolled his eyes, and without a second thought, Kathleen balled up her fist, pulled back, and clocked Harrison in the face. His head bobbed backward and returned upright with blood trickling out his nose.

"Shit!" he shouted.

Simon stepped between Kathleen and Harrison. "All right, take him away," Simon told Chase. Chase led Harrison to the Humvee, put him into the backseat, and closed the door.

Simon asked Kathleen, "Feel better?"

She answered, "Yeah. No. A little."

They laughed and hugged.

"Chase is alive," she giggled.

"Chase is alive," he confirmed.

# EPILOGUE

Kathleen Wood sat on Rocky Balboa, watching the water rush by. She had been sitting on the large rock for so long that her butt was numb.

Her shotgun leaned against Rocky. It was around noon and the sun shone in a clear sky, but it was only about twenty-five degrees out.

Looking down at the river, she noticed two or three inches from the edge a slight translucent layer of ice had formed. The sheet of ice looked so magical and fragile. Another wonderful act of nature she never got tired of witnessing, just like the night all the craziness started.

She closed her eyes and took a deep breath, concentrating on the smell of the river and the sound of running water. It calmed her senses.

She was almost in a meditative state when she heard something behind her. She snapped out of her trance, slid off the rock, grabbed the shotgun, and whipped around pointing the barrel toward the sound.

"It's just me," Chase said as he walked toward her holding two cups of hot cocoa. He held one cup out for her. She set the shotgun down, took the cup, and gave him a quick peck on the lips. He held out his hand for an assist onto Rocky, then he found a spot next to her.

So, tell me how it went," she inquired.

"Harrison was arraigned and held without bond because he was a flight risk. He cried like a baby during the hearing and all the news channels played it."

Kathleen laughed imagining seeing it on TV.

"His supporters are saying it's all a conspiracy to keep him from running for president."

She shrugged and said, "Of course they are. I guess the days of anything being bipartisan are long gone. No matter how damning the actions."

Chase continued, "Simon had the Idaho Air National Guard remove the helicopter from the cliff. David agreed to be a witness against Harrison in exchange for not being charged with blackmail. He's probably being interviewed right now, as we speak. Simon has people looking into it, but no one seems to know if Greg is really dead or not.

Kathleen took a sip from her cocoa. She turned and looked at Chase. She lifted her other hand and touched a faint scab on his temple, "Well, you're not dead."

"No, I'm not."

"I'm glad," she said as they locked eyes.

Light snowflakes began to fall from the sky, and they kissed.


The End

# ACKNOWLEDGMENTS

Thank you to my wife, Tauna for her endless support.

Thank you to my family whose love, support, and encouragement are never failing. My attorney, Jay Gustavsen, TEN-41 Publishing, Dennis Mansfield, Rich Summers, and Ashely Brock for a great cover. Thank you to my editor/formatter and so much more, Stacey Smekofske.

And thank you to those who continue to read my stories, thank you.

---

The idea for this story came to me about five years ago. I jotted the rough idea down, and over time, I continued to work on it here and there. About six months ago I put it on the front burner. I'm so glad I did. The story started to flow, and I'm pleased with where we ended up. I hope you enjoy it too.

Buckle up, there will be Blood in the Snow.

# ABOUT RYAN PACHECO

Ryan Pacheco is a Best Selling Author. Besides *Blood in the Snow*, Ryan has authored the Isaac Jones Political Thriller series, the Alexander Stone crime series, *Benghazi and Beyond*, *Targeted*, *Earth's Dimensions*, and *The Heist*.

When Ryan isn't home surrounded by the picturesque scenery of the Treasure Valley, he enjoys traveling. He takes pleasure in eating at nice restaurants and is a self-proclaimed foodie.

You can follow what Ryan is doing at www.RyanPacheco.us

# TITLES BY RYAN PACHECO

## TARGETED
### AN ISAAC JONES THRILLER

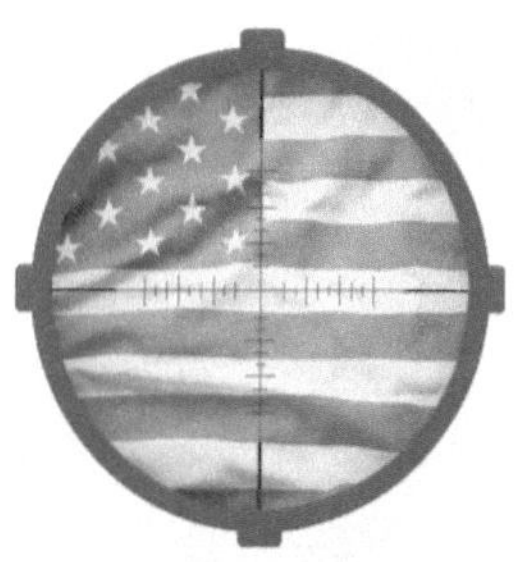

**RYAN PACHECO**
AND DENNIS MANSFIELD